ALSO BY A.B. YEHOSHUA

The Continuing Silence of a Poet:
The Collected Stories of A.B. Yehoshua

The Lover

A Late Divorce

Five Seasons

Mr Mani

Open Heart

A Journey to the End of the Millennium

The Liberated Bride

A WOMAN IN JERUSALEM

A Passion in Three Parts

A.B. YEHOSHUA

Translated from the Hebrew by
Hillel Halkin

HALBAN
LONDON

First published in Great Britain by
Halban Publishers Ltd.
22 Golden Square
London W1F 9JW
2006

www.halbanpublishers.com

A CIP catalogue record for this book is available from the British Library.

ISBN 1870015 98 3

Originally published in Hebrew as
Shelihuto shel ha-memuneh al mash'abe enosh
(The Mission of the Human Resources Director)
by Hakibbuz Hameuchad, Tel Aviv, 2004.
Copyright © 2004 by A. B. Yehoshua
Translation copyright © 2006 Hillel Halkin

Typeset by Computape Typesetting, North Yorkshire
Printed in Great Britain by Mackays of Chatham
a member of The CPI Group

In memory of our friend Dafna, killed by the bomb
on Mount Scopus, in the summer of 2002

PART ONE

The Manager

Even though the manager of the human resources division had not sought such a mission, now, in the softly radiant morning, he grasped its unexpected significance. The minute the extraordinary request of the old woman, who stood in her monk's robe by the dying fire, was translated and explained to him, he felt a sudden lifting of his spirits, and Jerusalem, the shabby, suffering city he had left just a week ago, was once more bathed in a glow of importance, as it had been in his childhood.

And yet the origins of his unusual mission lay in a simple clerical error brought to the company's attention by the editor of a local Jerusalem weekly, an error that could have been dealt with by any reasonable excuse and brief apology. However, fearing that such an apology – which might indeed have laid the matter to rest – would be deemed inadequate, the stubborn eighty-seven-year-old owner of the company had demanded a more tangible expression of regret from himself and his staff, a clearly defined gesture such as the one that had resulted in this journey to a distant land.

What had upset the old man so? Where had the almost religious impulse that drove him come from? Could it have been inspired by the grim times that the country, and above all Jerusalem, were going through, which he had weathered unharmed; so that his financial success, as other businesses foundered, called for vigilance in warding off the public criticism that now, ironically, was about to be aired in newsprint of which he himself was the supplier? Not that the reporter, a political radical and eternal doctoral candidate with the restraint of a bull in this intimate china shop of a city – whose scathing feature article would break the story – was aware of all this when he wrote the piece, otherwise he would have toned it down. Yet it was the paper's editor and publisher, loath to ruin a colleague's weekend with an unpleasant surprise that might spoil their business relations, who had decided, after taking a look at the story and its accompanying photograph of the torn, bloodstained pay slip found in the murdered woman's shopping bag, to let the old man respond in the same issue.

Nor was it really such a shocking exposé. Nevertheless, at a time when pedestrians were routinely exploding in the streets, troubled consciences turned up in the oddest places. And so at the end of that particular working day, when the human resources manager, having promised his ex-wife that he would leave the office on time to be with their only daughter, had tried to evade the owner's summons, the old man's long-serving office manager had refused to let him. Sensing her boss's agitation, she'd hastened to advise the resource manager to put his family duties aside.

On the whole, relations between the two men were good. They had been so ever since the resource manager, then in the sales division, had unearthed several Third World markets for the company's new line of paper and stationery products. And so, when his manager's marriage was on the rocks, in part because of his frequent travels, the old man had reluctantly agreed to appoint him temporary head of the human resources division, a job that would allow him to sleep at home every night and try to repair the damage. Yet the hostility engendered by his absence was only distilled into a more concentrated poison by his presence, and the chasm between them – at first psychological, then intellectual, and finally sexual – continued to grow of its own accord. Now that he was divorced, all that kept him from returning to his old job, which he had liked, was his determination to stay close to his daughter.

As soon as he'd appeared in the doorway of the owner's spacious office, where the elegantly muted light never changed with the time of day or year, the article due to appear in the local weekly was dramatically hurled at him.

"An employee of *ours*?" The resource manager found that hard to credit. "Impossible. I would have known about it. There must be some mistake."

The owner did not answer. He simply held out the galleys, which the resource manager read quickly while still standing.

The odious article was entitled "The Shocking Inhumanity Behind Our Daily Bread." Its subject was a woman in her forties found critically wounded after a bombing in the Jerusalem market the week before. Her only identifying mark had been a pay slip issued by the company. For two days she had fought for her life in the hospital without any of her employers or fellow workers taking the slightest interest in her. Even after her death, she had lain in the hospital morgue abandoned and unidentified, her fate unmourned and her burial unprovided for. (There followed a brief description of the company and its large, well-known bakery, founded at the beginning of the twentieth century by the owner's grandfather and recently augmented by the new line of paper products.) Two photographs accompanied the text. One, taken years ago, was an old studio portrait of the owner; the other was of the human resources manager. It was dark and blurry, evidently snapped recently, without his knowledge. The caption noted that he owed his position to his divorce.

"The little weasel!" the resource manager muttered. "What a nasty smear . . ."

But the old man wanted action, not complaints. It wasn't the tone of the article that bothered him – yellow journalism was the fashion nowadays – but its substance. Since the editor had been kind enough to allow them to respond immediately, which might defuse charges that would only gain ground if uncontested for a week, they had better find out who the woman was and why no one knew anything about her. In fact – why not? – they should contact the weasel himself to see what he knew. It was anyone's guess what he meant to reveal next.

In a word, the human resources manager would have to drop everything and concentrate on this. Surely he understood that his responsibility was to deal not just with vacations, sick leaves, and retirements, but with death as well. If the article were to be published without a satisfactory response from them, its accusations of inhumanity and callous greed might arouse public protests that would affect their sales. After all, theirs wasn't just any bakery: the proud name of its founder was affixed to every loaf that left the premises. Why give their competitors an unfair edge?

"An unfair edge?" The human resources manager snorted. "Who cares about such things? And especially in times like these . . . "

"I care." The owner replied irritably. "And especially in times like these."

The resource manager bowed his head, folded the article, and stuck it matter-of-factly in his pocket, anxious to escape before the old man blamed him not only for keeping flawed records but for the bomb attack too. "Don't worry," he said with a reassuring smile. "I'll make this woman my business first thing tomorrow morning."

The tall, heavyset, expensively dressed, old man sat up, very pale, in his chair. His great pompadour of ancient hair swelled in the muted light like the plumes of a royal pheasant. His hand gripped his employee's shoulder with the full force of his threatened reputation. "Not tomorrow morning," he said slowly and with painstaking clarity. "Tonight. This evening. Now. No time to waste. I want all this cleared up before dawn. In the morning we'll send the paper our response."

"This evening? Now?" The resource manager was startled. He was sorry, but it was too late for that. He was in a hurry. His wife — his ex-wife, that is — was out of town and he had promised to look after their daughter and drive her to her dance class; what with all the bus bombings, they didn't want her taking public transport. "What's the hurry?" he asked. "The damn paper comes out on Fridays. It's only Tuesday. There's plenty of time."

But the owner was too worried about his humanity to relent. No, there was no time at all. The paper, distributed free with the weekend editions of the national tabloids, went to press on Wednesday night. If their response wasn't in by then, it would have to wait another week; meanwhile they would be open to all kinds of accusations. If the resource manager didn't wish to take care of this — and thoroughly — let him say so. There was no problem finding someone else – perhaps to run the human resources division, too . . .

"Just a minute. I didn't mean to . . . " The casually delivered ultimatum stung and bewildered him. "What am I supposed to do with my daughter? Who'll take care of her? You've met her mother," he added bitterly. "She'll murder me . . . "

"That's who'll take care of her," the owner interrupted, pointing to his office manager, who turned red at the thought of being entrusted with the chore.

"What do you mean?"

"What do you think I mean? She'll drive your daughter and look after her like her own child. And now let's roll up our sleeves and prove that we're as human as the weasel . . . that we care. For God's sake, my good man, is there any choice? No, there isn't."

2

"Yes, sweetheart. Yes, dear, I understand. I know you don't need to be driven. But please, do it for your mother's sake. And for mine. It's best to let this woman take you to your dance class and bring you back. There isn't any choice. There simply isn't . . . "

His cajoling tone over the telephone, meant to placate a disappointed daughter who wanted a father not a driver, sounded rather like his boss's.

"You're right," he confessed a minute later, this time fending off his ex-wife, who, informed by his daughter of his change of plans, had called to accuse him of dereliction of duty. "I admit it. I did promise. But something awful has happened. Try to be human. An employee of ours was killed in a bombing and I have to take care of the details. You don't want me to lose my job, do you? There isn't any choice . . . "

This lack of choice first announced by the owner would echo within him like a comforting mantra – and not just on that first long, meandering night, by the end of which he was conjuring the dead. No, in the strange days following – on the

7

funeral expedition that same weekend to the steppes of a far country, in the hardest moments of indecision, the worst junctures of crisis and uncertainty – he would rally his companions with the same phrase. It was like a banner in battle, the beacon from a lighthouse, flickering in the dark to give them courage and direction. There was no choice. They had to see it through to the end, even if this meant retracing their steps to the beginning.

With that simple phrase he rounded up and cowed his secretary, who had left work early without permission. It was useless for her to argue over the telephone that she had already sent the nanny home and had no one to look after her baby. The owner's determination to be human had inspired him too. "There's no choice. You can bring the baby here and I'll look after it. We have to trace that woman with the pay slip as quickly as possible. You're the only one who can do it."

And to top it all, a fierce, blustery rain descended at that exact moment, an early portent of the bountiful winter that befell us that year. It was a winter on which we pinned a desperate hope: that more than all our policemen and security guards, it might cool the suicidal zeal of our enemies. The dry countryside turned green and the earth was covered with grasses and flowers whose scent we had forgotten. Not a word of protest was uttered against the torrents of fresh water that flooded our pavements and tied up traffic on our roads, for we knew that not all would be lost. Enough would find its way to hidden aquifers to comfort us when the hot, dry summer returned.

When his secretary, bundled up and dripping wet, arrived with the first brushstrokes of evening, the human resources manager thought at first that she had left the baby at home. Then she folded her umbrella, took off her yellow poncho, and slipped out of her big fur coat, he saw that strapped to her was a carrier in which, curiously scrutinizing him, sat a lusty, red-cheeked infant with a giant dummy in its mouth. "What kind of a way is that to pack a baby?" he asked in surprise. "It could have choked in there." His secretary, her brusque tone unlike her customary nine-to-five one, retorted "Trust me," and set the baby down on the rug with a fresh dummy. The

8

little creature glanced around as if looking for a suitable destination, spat out its new mouthpiece, turned on its stomach, and began to crawl with surprising speed, the dummy clutched in its hand. "*He's* all yours," said the secretary still in an irritated yet intimate tone. "You said you'd look after him."

She took the article and read it slowly. Then, examining from different angles the blurred photograph of the pay slip found in the dead woman's possession, she asked the manager who, bemused, was watching the crawling baby, "Just when did all this happen?" Informed of the date of the bombing, she hazarded a guess that the woman had left her job at least a month earlier. Stub or no stub, she had ceased to be their employee. The whole nasty article was fraudulent.

The resource manager, his eyes still on the baby (who had reached the door leading to the corridor, and whose progress he was thinking perhaps he ought to block), replied dolefully:

"Fraudulent, shmaudulent. We have to find out who she was and why no one knows anything about her. If she left her job or was fired, why was she still on the payroll? There has to be a record of it somewhere. Let's get to work. We have no time to waste."

He turned to follow the baby – who, briefly stymied by the darkness in the corridor, had rapidly resumed his course and was now heading for the door of the owner's office.

No wonder they're ready to climb the Himalayas by the time they're twenty, the resource manager thought as he trailed after it. Now and then the infant stopped without warning and sat up pertly, as if to reflect before continuing. The stocky man walking behind it – of average height and close to forty, with the first streaks of grey in his military crew cut – felt overcome by a deep, weary dejection. He was oddly resentful of the anonymous woman who had gone shopping without so much as an ID card for the sole purpose of making him – hungry, thirsty, and exhausted from a long day's work – responsible for finding out who she was.

The baby reached the end of the corridor and halted in

front of the office of the owner – who, secure in the knowledge that his reputation was in good hands, was now enjoying a quiet dinner. The door, elegantly upholstered in black leather to guard the secrets exchanged behind it, posed a challenge; the baby, dummy still clutched in one hand, was rapping eagerly on the barrier when the secretary called out in triumph that the mystery had been solved. *I run a tight ship after all*, the human resources manager reflected, scooping up the infant before it could protest and bearing it aloft like a hijacked aeroplane to its mother, on whose brightly coloured computer screen had appeared not only the personal résumé but also a blonde beaming woman, no longer young.

"Bingo!" she declared. "In a minute I'll give you a printout. Now that I know the date on which she started work, I'll even find your job interview with her."

"*I* interviewed her?" The surprised manager was still holding the baby, whose tiny little hand was crumpling his ear.

"Who else? Your first directive on taking the job last July was that no one was to be hired or fired without your knowledge."

"But what did she do here?" The discovery that he had had a connection to the murdered woman made the resource manager uneasy. "Where did she work? Who was in charge of her? What does your computer say?"

The computer was not outspoken about these things. Its code showed only that the woman had been attached to a cleaning team that moved among the company's different branches. "In that case," the manager murmured sadly, "she must have fallen between the branches when she died . . . "

The secretary, a long-time employee to whom the company owed several improvements (it was she who had changed the name *personnel department* to *human resources division* and introduced the computerized scanning of faces), begged to differ. "No one disappears around here," she told the manager, who was still rather dependent on her. "Every employee, even the lowliest cleaning woman, has someone to make sure they punch in and do their job."

She was so preoccupied with the administrative and perhaps even moral aspects of the matter that she seemed to have forgotten all about the home she hadn't wanted to leave, the children waiting for supper, and the raging winter storm. As if the owner's impugned humanity had infected her too, she was now energetically engaged in her next task, extracting last summer's job interview from a filing cabinet as unerringly as she had accessed the dead woman on her computer. Stapled to the interview was a brief medical report from the company's doctor. She punched holes in both, did the same with the article and photographs, attached them all together with a clip, and slipped them into a yellow folder that she handed to the manager as Exhibit A – scant evidence, to be sure, but still a start.

The baby began to bawl. Taking it from the resource manager's arms, the secretary suggested he might want to peruse the file in his office, or look away at any rate while she attended to her child. It had to be fed; otherwise it would not leave them in peace to determine who was to blame for this mess. Before she had even finished the sentence, the top button of her blouse was open, her breast halfway out.

3

At least we now have a clue to work with, the resource manager thought with satisfaction as he entered his office and cleared his desk to make room for the folder. Although there was no need to linger over the snapshot of this forty-eight-year-old woman, her open face and light eyes gave him pause. An exotic arch, northern European or Asiatic, ran from each eyelid to the nose. The neck, exposed in all its perfection, was long and rounded. For a moment he forgot that she was no longer a living being, that nothing was left of her but a bureaucratic indifference to her fate.

He felt an urge to phone the owner and boast of his swift progress, then thought better of it as a new wave of annoyance swept over him. In his obsession with the public's image of his humanity, the old man had ridden roughshod over the rights of three employees. Let him stew in the juices of his maligned name a little longer! Why give him the pleasure of thinking that his request had been easy, even enjoyable, to carry out?

He glanced at a page listing the woman's personal details and turned to her employment form, quailing slightly at the sight of her CV, which had been written not in her own hand, as was customary, but in his. He had evidently recorded her words verbatim, as though taking down a confession.

My name is Ragayev. Yulia Ragayev, mechanical engineer. I have diploma. But I was not born in city, was born in small village. Far away. Far, far from big city. My mother lives in village still. I have son too, big boy now, thirteen years. His father engineer also. I am not longer with him. Good man but we separate. I leave him for other man, good too. More old than him. But not so much. Sixty years. His wife is long time dead and he come to work in our city, in our factory. There we meet. I want much he should come to Jerusalem and he say yes, so we come here, I, him, and boy. But he not find good job for important engineer. He not want stay. Why someone like him just clean street or be guard or something? He go back – not to my city, his. He has daughter and granddaughter there. I, no. I want to stay in Jerusalem. Maybe is good here. Because Jerusalem I like. Is interesting place. If I go back, I never come again. First son is here too, but then father say is too dangerous and he must leave. Okay, I say, he go back. I stay and try Jerusalem. Is sometimes good, sometimes bad. I work for who need me, even though I have engineer's diploma. What does it matter, maybe my son come back. Is such my situation. Now mother in village want to come to Jerusalem, too. Well, we will see, maybe she come.

The next document was a signed statement by the woman, this time dictated by the human resources manager himself. *I, Yulia Ragayev, holder of temporary resident card no. 836205, agree to work at any job I am assigned to, including night shifts.*

Beneath this, in large letters, was her signature, followed by his comments:

This woman has temporary residence status. She has no family, looks healthy, and makes a good impression. She seems highly motivated. Although first placement should be in a service job, her professional training may enable her at some point to move to the production line at the bakery or in to the paper-and-stationery division.

Beneath this was a laconic note from the doctor: *No special health problems. Cleared for all work.*

At the reception desk, the secretary was losing no time. While nursing her baby, she efficiently telephoned instructions for the preparation of supper for her children and husband. Then, launching a private investigation of her own, she briskly asked the day shift supervisor over the intercom whether he was aware that a cleaning woman, one Yulia Ragayev, had been absent from work. Without mentioning the woman's fate, she asked whether she had resigned or been dismissed and, in either case, why the human resources division hadn't been informed.

Listening from his desk through the open door, the resource manager picked up the receiver in time to catch the day shift supervisor's reply. Yes, he had a vague memory of the employee in question and had even noticed she was missing. But it would be better to ask the night shift supervisor, who had been her superior. Irked by the tone of this mere secretary, he advised her to have the resource manager contact the night shift supervisor directly.

The mere secretary, however, was not put off by such short shrift. Politely ending the conversation without ever mentioning the woman's death, as if that were her trump card, she curtly summoned the resource manager. Outside her regular work hours, so it seemed, she was the one who gave orders.

He stepped out of his office to find the nursing successfully accomplished, its certificate of completion a pungent-smelling nappy. While she watched her baby, pink-cheeked and contented, thrash its legs in benediction, the secretary preened herself on her intuition. "You'll see," she said. "Even though we issued that woman another pay packet, she was no longer employed by us at the time of the bombing. You can tell that asshole of a reporter and his charming boss that it's they who

13

should apologize to us. They can take their 'shocking in-humanity' and shove it. And while you're at it, tell your own boss to calm down." She threw a last glance at the cleaning woman on her screen, and said, "It's too bad. She was an attractive woman," then switched off the computer.

"Attractive?" The resource manager frowned and opened the folder for another look at the photograph. "I wouldn't say that. If she were that good-looking, I'd have remembered her."

The secretary did not reply at once. Deftly putting on a fresh nappy, she threw the old one in the bin, strapped on the carrier, placed her baby in it, slipped into her big fur coat, and threw on the crackling yellow poncho. The baby vanished from sight. With a sharp glance at the human resources manager, as if seeing him for the first time, she said, "Abso-lutely. More than good-looking. Beautiful. If you didn't notice when you hired her, that's because you live inside yourself like a snail. All you see of beauty or goodness is its shadow ... But why argue about someone who's no longer with us? What will either of us prove? I'd better go with you to the bakery to ask the night shift supervisor how an employee can disappear and no one bother to notify us."

He regarded her affectionately, pleased with her down-to-earthness. Taking his windcheater from the hanger, he put it on and had already turned out the light when it occurred to him to ask if there was anything cold in the fridge.

"You want a cold drink *now*?" She opened the little refrigerator, in which there was nothing but a carton of long-life milk for coffee.

There wasn't any choice. Fighting back nausea, he slowly sipped the cold liquid.

4

Whereas an hour ago she had argued and pleaded against having to return to the office, now, wrapped in her winter gear, with a satisfied baby snuggled close to her, she was in

14

high spirits as she trotted beside him along the paved path leading from the administration building to the huge, windowless bakery with its pencil-thin chimneys. From the overhang of the handsome tiled roof cascaded not one storm but many, each more torrential than the last. It was as if the earth, having lost all hope of emptying the sky in a single downpour, was draining it in stages.

The human resources manager was thinking of the office manager, now parenting his daughter. He felt confident that she would be at the dance studio on time to keep her ward from taking a perilous bus home; nowadays, you couldn't trust even the rain to deter a would-be bomber who had said his farewell prayers and set out to kill and be killed. How curious, he reflected, moved by the thought, that a foreign cleaning woman remembered by no one could cause a wave of solidarity among the company's employees. In a gesture he was generally careful to avoid, he laid a friendly hand on his secretary's shoulder while shouting above the wind:

"I tell you, you'll smother that baby yet!"

"Not on your life!" the secretary shouted back with full assurance, wiping raindrops from her face. "I can feel his every breath. Right now he's sending you his warmest regards."

Meanwhile, as dusk fell in that rain squall, our entire night shift arrived. There were ninety of us, men and women: silo workers, millers, flour sifters, dough kneaders, lab technicians with their yeast and additives. The technicians roamed the large work spaces, checking the dials that monitored the baking cycle in the huge ovens — great sealed steel compartments beside which stood the production crews, supervising the golden loaves to make sure they stayed on their conveyor belts. And there were also the collectors, the sorters, and the packers of the products that the assembly line spewed out: whole and sliced loaves, pitas, bagels, rolls, challahs, flatbreads, croutons, bread crumbs. In a shed outside, the forklift operators were noisily joined by the lorry drivers, who would transport the goods all over the country. The late-to-arrive cleaning crews were also pressed into action, dressed like the rest of us in white smocks and net caps that would keep the least strand of hair from getting into the circulating dough. Swinging

15

their buckets and dragging their brooms, they scrubbed the burned crusts from the day shift's baking pans while sneaking a glance at the wall clock to make sure that Time was alive and well and would not desert them before the night was over.

It was then that we saw the two dripping wet people from personnel – a sturdy man and a stout woman in a black fur coat and a yellow poncho. Before they could say a word we stopped them at the entrance and made them put on caps.

The human resources manager donned the cap willingly and drifted towards the warmth of the steel ovens in the middle of the work floor. Through his old job he knew the paper-and-stationery branch across the street very well and preferred to meet with its workers on the premises; the employees of the bakery, on the other hand, he generally received in his office when they came to ask for a pay increase or discuss some problem. Now, as he faced the bakery's many ovens with their long, mysterious cycles that churned out endless crates of breads and rolls, he was reminded of those times he was dispatched as a child by his mother to make some purchase in the local grocery.

Nevertheless, on this rainy evening he felt grateful for the fragrant warmth that greeted him at the end of this long workday, ahead of which stretched a dizzying night. His anger at his ex-wife and feelings of guilt towards his daughter were muted by the familiar sight of the dough rolling by at eye level on its way to the sorting and leavening stations and from there to the hidden fires. While pleasurably taking in the bakery's sounds, smells, and sights – as though he had a share in his secretary's lusty baby – he proudly watched its golden head emerge from the depths of her fur coat. Some workers, their curiosity piqued by the unexpected visit, hurried to get the night shift supervisor, while the secretary warned him in a stern whisper not to mention the death that had brought them here. It, too, she seemed to think, was small enough to be hidden beneath a coat.

The supervisor, a tall, lanky, swarthy man of about sixty appeared quickly. Besides his smock and cap, he had on a blue technician's apron. There was apprehension in his fine-featured, sensitive face. A sudden visit from the personnel division at this time of day couldn't possibly bode well.

"Does a cleaning woman named Yulia Ragayev still work here?" the secretary asked, hurrying to pose the question before the resource manager could ignore her warning and blurt out that the woman had been murdered, thus putting the supervisor on his guard. "She's been missing from our roster for a month."

The supervisor reddened. He seemed to sense a trap, though he could hardly guess that death was lurking in it. With a worried glance at the cleaning crew crowding around him, he signalled them to disperse. Though they took a few backward steps, like sleepwalking bears, they continued to surround him, intrigued by the situation and the mysterious baby.

"Ragayev?" The lanky man spread his hands and regarded them as if the missing worker might have been hiding there. "Actually . . . no. Yulia left a while ago."

The intimacy with which he uttered the dead woman's first name gave the human resources manager a start. The secretary persisted, stubborn as an attack dog. *Left? How? Of her own accord? Or was she laid off? And if so, why? For what infraction? Who replaced her?* None of the human resources division's records showed a decrease in the number of cleaning personnel – and in any case, begging the night shift supervisor's pardon, a long-serving employee like him should know that any change in the work force had to be reported and approved. This was necessary to avoid confusion and damage.

"Damage?" The swarthy man scoffed. "What damage can a temporary cleaning woman's departure do?"

The resource manager, unprepared for the secretary's cross-examination, was waiting to see when she would reveal that the woman had died. She was taking her time about it. She gave the supervisor, towards whom she appeared to have developed a strange antagonism, a suspicious look, as if he were her prime suspect.

"What damage?" she repeated. "Imagine our predicament if a former employee got into trouble with the law while still on our payroll, let alone our continuing to pay social security and employment taxes for someone who no longer works here . . ."

The man was indeed behaving oddly. Rather than giving a straight answer, he kept asking why he was being questioned. On a rainy night like this? After hours? He knew that the woman hadn't lodged a complaint.

"What makes you so sure?" asked the secretary.

Because it wasn't like her. She wasn't the complaining type.

"Then why did you fire her?"

Who said she'd been fired?

"Then what happened? Why are you beating around the bush?"

Was the night shift supervisor afraid of being caught out? Instead of replying, he demanded to know, yes or no, whether they had been in touch with the woman.

"Not yet," the secretary said, flashing the manager a conspiratorial smile. "But we may be."

This time she's gone too far, thought the resource manager. Yet he continued to keep silent. The golden light and shadows of the bakery playing over his net cap, made him look like an old woman.

"Look," the supervisor said, backing down. "It doesn't matter. I was only asking." If they spoke to the woman, she would confirm his account. Although she hadn't been fired, she hadn't exactly quit either. It was more of . . . a termination of employment by mutual agreement. Of course, he should have filed a report, but this was only a formality. Neither the management nor the union, after all, had the right to oppose a temporary employee's being laid off during her trial period. Not that she hadn't been a good worker. In fact, she had performed her job flawlessly, even though it was far beneath her professional level. "You people in personnel sent her to be a cleaning woman not realizing you were looking at a trained engineer." This was why he had counselled her to look for better work. It had pained him to see her making the rounds every night with a bucket and mop.

But while this explanation, straightforward at last, should have been enough for the delegation from personnel, it failed to satisfy the ferretlike secretary. She squared her shoulders to face the supervisor, her hair straying from her net cap and her fur coat opened to reveal her baby, its arms flailing, its legs chugging like an engine.

"So that's it! You fired a perfectly satisfactory worker because you felt sorry for her. You might at least have asked whether we could find her a more suitable job elsewhere, perhaps in paper and stationery . . . "

But the supervisor had had enough. Shooing away the workers still clustered around him, he told his interrogators that he was needed on another floor. He still didn't understand what was wanted of him. All this couldn't be just because of some needlessly paid social security. If that was the problem, they could deduct the sum from his next pay packet and be done with it.

Why, the resource manager wondered, don't I say something to stop this whirling dervish of a secretary from attacking a senior employee? The warmth and good smells of the bakery had so drugged his senses that he thought he must be dreaming when he heard the supervisor ask again, "What's going on? Has she been in touch with you? Tell me the truth," and his secretary replied, "As a matter of fact, she has. But not in the way you think."

It was time to speak up before it was too late. "She was killed in last week's suicide bombing," the resource manager declared.

As if the belt of explosives detonated in the market had gone off a second time, the supervisor turned red, staggered backward, and clutched his head.

"I don't believe it . . . "

"You'd better," the secretary said, with what appeared to be genuine pleasure.

This time the resource manager cut her short. As simply as

possible, he told the supervisor about the article that was to appear and the owner's worry that it might hurt sales.

"You've got us into a fix with your private termination of employment," he concluded sadly. "But at least we know now that she wasn't working for us when she died. That means she wasn't our responsibility."

Although the night shift supervisor was clearly stunned, the secretary's hostility towards him remained unabated. The resource manager once more laid a hand on her shoulder and said, gently, "That wraps it up, then. It's late. And this rain shows no sign of slowing down. We've found out what we needed to know. Thanks for your help. I can take it from here. Your children are waiting for you ... "

Feeling oddly emotional, he planted a kiss on the baby's head to thank him for behaving so well.

The little boy shut his eyes blissfully and let the dummy drop from his mouth.

Having finished playing detective, the secretary buttoned her fur coat. She removed her net cap and handed it to the supervisor, who carefully folded it and put it in his pocket as if it were the last vestige of the death he had just learned of. The secretary was now engaged in watching the long spirals of the assembly lines with their slowly rising dough on its way to the hot ovens. Sobered by the immensity of it all, and by the rank of the man she had been questioning, she smiled ruefully and inquired whether, as an employee in personnel, she had the same right as the bakery workers to a free loaf of bread every day.

The supervisor smiled at his inquisitor's request. He took a large bag, filled it with three different kinds of bread, two packages of rusks, and one each of croutons and breadcrumbs, and asked a worker to take it to the secretary's car. Would the resource manager like some, too?

The resource manager thought it over and replied,

"Come to think of it, why not?"

5

Taking one loaf of bread, he firmly declined a second, as if this might involve a dangerous impropriety. Yet instead of leaving the bakery with his secretary, he stayed by the side of the supervisor, who hurried off to another, even larger work space with an even bigger oven. Two technicians were waiting for permission to light it, a process involving a battery of freestanding switches, dials, and lifts. The supervisor, hesitant and uncertain only a minute ago, now issued crisp, authoritative orders, to which the oven, like a trained circus animal awakened from its sleep, responded with a low growl. Enveloped in a fragrant warmth, the resource manager watched the workers harmoniously performing their tasks. He felt a pang of envy. How much better it was on a stormy night like this to work with simple matter than with fragile, vulnerable human life. Any error here could be corrected by pressing a button.

The night shift supervisor didn't like being followed around. Exactly what, he asked the human resources manager once the oven was lit – its steady drone accompanied by a thin whine – was still bothering him? Hadn't he, the supervisor, promised that in the morning, at the end of his shift, he would go to the owner's office, admit his mistake, and offer to have the money deducted from his pay packet? When the human resources manager, his attention drawn to a fresh conveyor belt that had begun to clatter, replied that they should wait to see whether the weekly called off the article, the supervisor declared morosely:

"They'll never call off anything."

"Why not? It's obvious that the woman had nothing to do with us at the time of her death."

"Don't be naïve. It doesn't matter if she did or didn't. That journalist isn't going to give up his story. If we correct him on one thing, he'll get us somewhere else. We should let him publish. Why make a fuss? People pick up local weeklies for the restaurant reviews and used-car ads, that's all. And even if a few souls do read it, they'll forget it before they've finished . . . "

The manager, suddenly aware of a new contradiction, asked: "If you felt so sorry for her, why didn't you wait for her to find a new job first?"

"How do you know she didn't?"

"Because she was broke. There was nothing in her shopping bag but rotten fruit."

"That's ridiculous." The supervisor flushed. "Who can tell after a bombing what's rotten and what isn't? Take my advice and drop it. Don't mess with a rotten journalist. In the end, no one will remember . . . "

The manager regarded the supervisor in silence. Before the night is out I'll surprise the old man yet, he told himself, feverishly toying with a new thought. He removed his net cap and handed it to the supervisor, who stuck it in his pocket with the secretary's. Then, waving good night, he headed back through the large, warm work space and out to the administration building. At the exit he was besieged by the cleaning women, eager to hear about their co-worker's death. Yet what could he tell them? No more than they could tell him. It was a large bakery with many corners, and each one of them worked alone. The dead woman, a temporary who feared for her job, had worked harder than the rest of them and never stopped to chat with anyone.

Outside it was still stormy. A convoy of army trucks pulled into the bakery's large yard and arranged themselves in a hissing row at the loading platforms. The human resources manager fought a sudden urge to ask the workers if they, too, like the secretary, had found the woman beautiful. He didn't want to be wrongly suspected, especially concerning someone who was dead.

Lifting the collar of his thin overcoat, he ran back to the administration building.

6

He returned to his office. Once again he thought of informing the bakery's owner of his progress. Once again he refrained. He would keep his plans to himself and let the old man fret for his humanity.

He dialled the weekly and asked to speak to the editor. The man's secretary, sounding as efficient and energetic as his own, replied that her boss was away and would not be available for the next twenty-four hours. He was taking a badly needed break and had gone off to commune with himself, leaving even his cell phone behind. Perhaps she could help the caller?

Once again it struck the resource manager how keen some people were to step into their superiors' shoes. Introducing himself, he inquired discreetly whether she knew anything about the article.

Indeed, she knew all about it. In fact, she considered herself a party to the affair, having been the one to suggest to the editor that he warn his friend, the owner of the bakery. Moreover, it was she who had urged the old man to submit his explanation and apology by tomorrow, when it would have the greatest impact.

"But that's just it!" the resource manager said excitedly. "We're not apologizing for anything. We're only explaining." The entire accusation was based on a mistake. A preliminary investigation had revealed that the dead woman, although she had once worked at the bakery, had not been employed there at the time of the bombing. Hence the company and its human resources division had been neither callous nor negligent. If the editor had indeed left without his cell phone, which he rather doubted, he would advise her to wield the authority vested in her by cancelling the article's publication.

"Cancel it?" The secretary sounded as shocked as if she had been asked to cancel tomorrow's sunrise. Absolutely not. It was out of the question. And besides, what was the resource manager so worried about? The article would appear, with the company's response in a sidebar, and the weekly's readers would decide for themselves.

"But that's absurd!" the resource manager protested angrily. "Why expose your readers to more horror stories in times like these?"

The secretary stuck to her guns. With all due respect to the resource manager's desire to acquit his company of blame, she wasn't authorized to cancel or postpone an article without the author's permission. If it was that crucial, the resource manager should contact the author directly and convince him to make changes. He had all night long to do it in.

"That weasel?"

"Weasel?" Her surprise was gleeful, vivacious. "Ha, ha, I like that! Does that come from knowing him personally or just from his writing?"

"From having read this single, ridiculous piece."

"Well, you've captured him perfectly. He doesn't look like a weasel – far from it – but that's just what he is: quick, slippery, and able to crawl into any hiding place to attack you by surprise. But tell me," the editor's secretary went on as though declaring her credo, "who keeps us on our toes if not the weasels? Every newspaper needs at least one. Only one, though ... that's quite enough, ha, ha ... "

As a token of her appreciation, she was even ready to give him the weasel's phone number.

Seated in the dark, empty administration building, with the bantering conversation having got him nowhere, he lapsed into gloom. Why on earth was he being so stubborn? What was he fighting for? To cover up the night shift supervisor's blunder? Or was it to show the old owner that he, his former star salesman, was still on top of things and the last person who should ever be threatened with dismissal? Or – he could feel the thought grope its way to the surface – was it to reclaim the dignity of an engineer come from afar to be a cleaning woman in Jerusalem. To let her know – her and whoever had loved her – that her suffering and death hadn't gone unnoticed because of anyone's callousness?

He switched on his desk lamp and slowly studied her computer image. Was she beautiful? It was hard to tell. He shut the folder and phoned home to ask about the dance lesson.

There was no answer. His daughter's substitute parent could be reached only on her cell phone. Every bit as lively as the two secretaries, she told him in her faint British accent that the dance lesson had ended a quarter of an hour ago. They weren't yet back in the apartment because his daughter had left her homework at a friend's house and they had to drive there to retrieve it.

"Again? On a rainy night like this?"

"What can I do about it? The rain is indeed inconsiderate." But there was no reason to be upset, said the office manager, tactfully defending the child's inattentiveness. She was waiting for her in a nice café. In fact, she wasn't even alone, because her husband was co-parenting with her. He was sitting by her side right now, having a beer. The resources manager could take his time – all night, if he wanted – to answer the scurrilous charges. She and her husband were used to teenage girls. They had a granddaughter the same age in America.

"All night?" Her generosity with his time annoyed him. "What for? Everything is wrapped up." He would soon come home to release them, he said, proudly declaring that he had tracked the dead woman down. Her name was Ragayev and a short but successful interrogation in the bakery had revealed the "termination" of her job. Although the company had indeed issued the pay slip that had put the journalist on the scent, she was no longer employed there at the time of the bombing. He was going to try to have the article cancelled, which in the editor's absence meant contacting the author.

The office manager reacted enthusiastically. Cancellation was the best solution – far better than a response on their part. It was just the thing to restore the old man's peace of mind. "Insist on it," she urged the resource manager. "We're taking good care of your daughter. You promised to make this woman your business – do it. Get hold of the journalist now ..."

The manager sighed. "He's a real weasel," he said. "Once he sinks his teeth into someone, he won't let go. He's liable to dig deeper and find more than just a clerical error."

"Such as what?"

"How should I know? He'll come up with something. Maybe involving the night shift supervisor . . . "

"But why assume the worst?"

"Why doesn't *he* make the call? I'll bet he has the editor's cell phone number."

The office manager, however, knew her boss too well to agree to this. Clerical errors were not his strong point, and he was apt to grow confused or excited and make matters worse. And time was of the essence. The weekly was going to press tomorrow, and the old man was now in a restaurant, before going on to a concert.

"The hell he is! He's going to concerts and restaurants while we're defending his honour?"

The office manager, a positive thinker, sought to correct him. "It's the honour of us all. The proper functioning of your division is involved, too. Leave the old man alone. Let him have his music. How much longer will he enjoy life? You needn't worry. My husband and I are looking after your daughter."

Compassion for his child welled within him. Didn't the office manager agree she was adorable?

"She's a good girl." As always, the office manager was being honest. "She's just . . . in a world of her own. A bit disorganized. It's hard to tell what she wants. But don't worry. She'll find herself in the end . . . "

The resource manager shut his eyes tight.

7

Vying with the smug, lazy drawl on the cell phone was the sound of pounding music. The weasel must be at a wedding or a nightclub. Yet not even the background noise could keep the journalist from swearing roundly at his editor for having shown the company owner an advance copy of his article. "The man's a moral scoundrel and a traitor to his profession," he said. "Now I understand why the little bastard was in such a hurry to disappear." He had begun to fear a stab in the back the moment his photographer had pointed out that the bakery also ran a paper products division that sold newsprint to the weekly. "So what are you telling me?" he asked the resource manager. "That you deserve moral immunity for a good price on newsprint? Why can't your response wait a week? You're trying to kill my article. Are you really so scared of finding out how inhuman you are or are you just worried about losing business? If the latter, I can only say I'm amazed to find such innocent capitalists. I only wish someone would think of boycotting you because of me. You needn't worry, though. No one will. Who cares about the inhumanity of a big company when staying human nowadays is too much for anyone? People are so screwed up that they'll even admire you for being tough. And suppose some bleeding heart is upset – so what? You think he'll go from shelf to shelf in the supermarket boycotting your products? What crap! What's wrong with you? You must be awfully unsure of yourselves to be so sensitive about a minor accusation. Don't make a big issue of it. Say you're sorry; just apologize. Only please wait a week before doing it."

"No one is sorry and no one is apologizing or waiting," the manager answered, shouting to make himself heard above the music. "You've got it all wrong. The woman left her job a month ago. At the time of the bombing she was no longer in our employ, even though we kept her on the payroll by mistake. I've checked it all out. We had no way of knowing she was dead and no reason to know. We expect you to be fair and withdraw your article."

The weasel's smug drawl bespoke no such intention. "What does that have to do with it? Do you think you can salve your consciences by firing her retroactively? If she was carrying your pay slip when she was killed, she obviously thought she worked for you. What are you trying to prove with your double-talk? Of course you were responsible! You not only owe her an apology, you owe one to her friends and relatives, who might have given her a decent burial if they'd known. It's the least you can do for a solitary employee like her, whom I'm sure you exploited all you could. If you want to be forgiven, you'll have to promise our readers never to be such callous shits again – that's the only way they'll forget what I wrote ... "

The resource manager lost his temper.

"Nothing ever gets forgotten in this country. And before you go judging us and giving us orders, maybe you'll tell me how you got involved in all this. Why didn't the hospital get in touch with us directly after the stub was found? Why did the morgue contact the press and not us?"

"In the first place," the lazy drawl continued, "they didn't contact the press. They contacted me. And secondly, the emergency room had no time to deal with such matters because it was too busy fighting to save her life. She was kept in the morgue when she died because nobody claimed her body – and there, as I happen to know from other cases, she got lost in the shuffle between the police and the hospital. It's not a question of anyone deliberately shirking his duty. It's more one of not knowing how to deal with an anonymous corpse. It took several days for the morgue's director, who is an acquaintance of mine, to go through the shopping bag and find that stub among the rotten fruit ... And by the way, before I go on, why do you issue such skimpy pay slips, with not even the name of the recipient printed on them?"

"Because every one of our employees has a different financial arrangement. We don't want complaints or comparisons because of stubs falling into the wrong hands."

"Just what I thought!" the weasel chuckled. "Divide and rule! Conceal and exploit! It's typical of you people. But I'm getting off the subject ... To cut a long story short, the director of the morgue, being a pathologist and not a sociologist, didn't know what to do and asked my advice. Over the past year we've become friends because of some features I wrote about the hospital's treatment of bombing victims. I'm afraid he's become a rather uncritical believer in the power of the press ..."

"But why didn't *you* contact us when you saw the stub?"

"Because by then I was enraged by your callousness and decided to teach you a public lesson. This isn't the first time a large company like yours has turned its back on a menial or temporary employee killed or injured in a terrorist attack."

"Just listen to yourself!" the manager shouted, grasping at last how the story got started. "You accuse us of inhumanity – yet it was you who left that woman alone in the morgue to teach us a lesson we didn't need ..."

"What do you mean alone?" The weasel laughed in amusement. "She had plenty of company."

"You know what I mean. Unidentified. So you could run a juicy story."

"Now you listen to me!" By now the journalist had lost his temper, too. "In cases like this I always look for the general rule – and that's the arrogance of the haves who trample the have-nots. You needn't worry about that woman. As far as she's concerned, she can stay in the morgue for all eternity. I've seen corpses wait for weeks before being identified and buried. Some never even get that far. Don't forget that the morgue belongs to the university's medical school and that students use it for their anatomy lessons. All for the sake of science. A year ago I wrote a feature about it, complete with photographs – tasteful ones – all you could see were the corpses' silhouettes. The paper was afraid to publish even that."

"I don't believe it," the resource manager said bitterly. "If you're in favour of science, what is this whole crusade for the dignity of the dead?"

The wild music suddenly stopped.

"The dignity of the dead?" The weasel sounded truly startled. "Do you really think that's what I'm fighting for? You'll have to excuse me, mister, but you're missing the point. I thought you would have realized by now that I don't give a damn for the dead. The line between life and death is clear to me. The dead are dead. Whatever dignity we accord them, or fear or guilt we have about them, are strictly our own. They have nothing to do with it. I'd think that a personnel director like you would understand that if I feel pain or sorrow, it's for the anonymous living, not the undignified dead. You may think I'm a romantic or a mystic, but the 'shocking inhumanity' is yours. And so is the unforgivable ease with which you forget a worker who doesn't show up for work. What with all the unemployed out there, you'll find someone else, so why worry, eh? If I let her stay unidentified for a few days longer, it was only to shock our jaded readers."

"But that's just my point," the resource manager said. "You didn't care about her at all. You just wanted to build a case. It's the worst kind of muckraking."

"What else could I do?" The journalist let out a sigh. "Such are the times we live in. You can't sell an idea, no matter how passionately you believe in it, unless you serve it cooked up with a scandal. Believe me, if the editor weren't so squeamish I'd have sent the photographer to shoot that woman in the morgue, because the director there told me ... he said she's ... I mean was ... in his opinion ... a good-looking woman. Or special-looking, anyway ... "

The resource manager thought he would choke. "Good-looking? Special-looking? Incredible! How dare you talk that way? Such good friends you two, he gave you a peep show. Don't deny it! You make me want to puke ... "

"Calm down. Who said I saw her?"

"You're the scandal, not us." He was getting carried away. "You complain of our inhumanity, but you don't mind your friend abusing his position to tell you intimate things about the dead. A good-looking woman? Who gave him permission to discuss her? Is that any way to deal with a terror victim? Unbelievable! The man is sick – and you're his accomplice. I could file a complaint against both of you. Who are you to give victims marks for being beautiful or ugly? I felt nauseous from the moment I started reading your article. It's not only nasty, it's pathological ... "

There was a chuckle of satisfaction at the other end of the line.

"Suppose it is. Why shouldn't it be? When everything around us is collapsing, it's pathological to fight it." True, his friend's praise for the woman's beauty – the weasel was decent enough to admit it – was what had aroused his interest in the first place. But why was the human resources manager surprised? Now that he knew who she was, he surely remembered her.

"Remember her? Of course I don't." Once again something quailed in him at being linked to the dead woman. "How could I? Our firm employs, in both of its branches, 270 or 280 workers in three shifts. Who can remember every one of them?"

"Well, you might at least tell me her name. What was her job? There must be a photograph in her file that we can publish. Or are you saving it for your apology? It will pep up the story. Our readers will love it . . . "

"A photograph? Forget it! And you're not getting her name from me, either. You're not getting anything unless you promise to withdraw your article altogether, or at least to tone it down."

"But why should I? It's a solid piece of writing. The one thing I'm willing to do is investigate the whole matter more thoroughly. How can a company fire someone and still keep her on the payroll? I wouldn't mind looking into that . . . she deserves as much . . . "

"For what purpose? To tell more lies and make more mistakes? Tell me: When Jerusalem is burning, does any of this matter? I'm not even talking about your photographing me in the street without permission or dragging in my divorce as though it were of public interest, although that's one thing that at least you could have left out . . . "

"Why? Don't tell me it's fiction," the journalist said. "I've already told you: a little bit of harmless gossip can make a point better than all the generalizations in the world. The public deserves to know how jobs are handed out in big companies. And why doesn't it matter? People like to read about terror attacks. They're not abstract. They're close to home and could happen to them. We all put ourselves first. The next time you're in a café, look at the customers. Apart from their depression and resentment at the situation, you can see how delighted they are, all the same, to be alive ... Why are you so angry with me? I don't deserve it. If you were to meet me in person, you would remember that we were once in the same class at university, in an introductory lecture course on Greek philosophy. That's why it surprised me to discover that you were heading the company's personnel division. I wouldn't have imagined you in such a cut-and-dried job. I don't suppose it's coincidence that the poor woman got lost in all your paperwork. She must have been a cleaning woman or something ... "

"Something." The resource manager winced.

"Won't you at least tell me her name?" the journalist pleaded. "You obviously know it."

"I'm not telling you anything."

"You'll have to mention it in your apology anyway."

Feeling the weasel's teeth sink into his throat, the resource manager regretted having phoned him.

"No, we won't," he protested. "We're not divulging any details. In the end, we may even choose not to respond. You just want to make us look terrible, to keep hitting us below the belt. Why help you? You can crawl in the dark on all fours, mister weasel, you can crawl like a blind animal and eat dirt ... "

There was no surprise or anger at the other end of the line. Only a chuckle of satisfaction. The human resources manager hung up.

8

He was now not only bone-weary but hungry as well. Before calling home again to see if his daughter had arrived, he went to the men's room to freshen up. It was being cleaned by someone new, a young blonde woman he had never seen before. Startled by his appearance after office hours, she took a step back while he graciously signalled her to carry on and then went to the ladies' instead. There, on his secretary's initiative, a full-length mirror had been installed. Facing it in the stillness of the evening, he saw a thirty-nine-year-old man of average height and powerful build, with hair clipped short in boot-camp style – a vestige of his many years in the army. In recent months, he had not liked the way he looked. A gloom had settled over him, narrowing his eyes in an expression of vague injury. What's bothering you, he silently scolded the figure staring glumly back at him. Was it only the owner's self-indulgent concern for his humanity? Or was it also the prospect of his own photograph in the local weekly, accompanied by a cynical reference to his divorce? The journalist, he now realized, was more cunning than he had thought. Barring a clear apology, he would probe some more and come up with a new accusation for next week's instalment. Once he knew the woman's name, it would be only a matter of time before he got to her fellow workers. Anyone who could make friends in a morgue could make them in a bakery too. Someone there had already leaked the connection between his divorce and his new job. He was quite sure it wasn't his secretary. Not that his reputation mattered to her, but the human resources division's did.

He splashed his face with water while considering the option of not reacting to the article at all. An aloof silence might be the best strategy. But such a strategy would make the owner say he was dodging his duty, which was the last thing he wanted. He ran a small, fine-toothed comb through his crew cut, took a tube from his pocket and rubbed Vaseline on his chapped lips, and returned to the men's room, determined to find out who the new cleaning woman was and who had hired her. She was gone, vanished like a ghost.

The office manager knew it was him even before he said a word. "We're all fine," she reassured him gaily. "We're heading back to the car with all the homework, even her

33

assignments for the weekend. We'll get to work on it as soon as we get home. I'll help with the English and my husband will freshen up his maths. Would you like to say hello?"

His daughter's habitually estranged, defensive voice had a new, hopeful note. "Yes," she told him. "They're very nice and they've promised to help with my homework. You don't have to hurry."

She giggled and handed the phone to the office manager, who asked whether the article had been cancelled.

"Not a chance. I should never have brought it up with that creep. He not only won't retract a word, he's planning a second instalment."

"Well, take your time. You have all night. We'll be here with your daughter. We're not going anywhere . . . "

"I don't need all night," he said. "And I've begun to think of it in a different, more sensible light. Why don't we just let the article appear and sink it by not responding? If you give me the old man's cell phone number, I can catch him before the concert."

The office manager, however, was not about to expose her boss to such a half-baked idea, certainly not before a concert. Why throw in the towel? "Think it over," she said. "Don't make any rash decisions. Remember that you have all night . . . "

He was about to make a cutting remark about the "all night". but refrained out of consideration for his daughter. Lamely saying good night to her, he reached for his loaf of bread and held it up to smell its freshness. Should he return to the bakery to warn the night shift supervisor of the journalist's plans, or could that wait until tomorrow?

Although he had intended to take the loaf home with him, he couldn't resist tasting the bread. In the absence of a knife, he tore off a piece with his strong fingers and opened his secretary's fridge to look for something to put on it. Tucked away in the butter compartment he found a chunk of yellow cheese, and though sure she wouldn't mind his taking it, he shrank from the thought of having to apologize in the morning for invading her privacy. Her new, free tone towards him and the night shift supervisor was bad enough without letting a chunk of cheese further lower the barrier he had erected between them, especially in the past months, since he had been single again.

He bit into the plain, dry white bread and found it tasty. Was it the same bread he was used to eating at home? Had his former wife looked for the bakery's label in the supermarket and bought it as a gesture of solidarity? Once all this was over, he intended to demand a free daily loaf for all the administration workers. He tore off another piece, opened the thin folder, and, chewing noisily, read for the third time the CV dictated to him by the woman, now dead.

The computer printout provided him with the date and place of her birth and her address in Jerusalem. Hoping to form a better notion of the beauty that had eluded him, he bent to take a closer look at the digital face and long, swan-like neck. Was the secretary right? Did he live inside himself like a snail while beauty and goodness passed like shadows? Even if he did, she needed to be taken down a peg. In the army he had had a reputation for keeping his female soldiers in line – until that is, he married one.

He shut the folder, tore off a third piece of bread, and went to the cabinet to get the file of the night shift supervisor. Bulky and tattered, it contained a pre-computer age black-and-white photograph of a handsome young man, a technician wearing the uniform of the Army Ordnance Corps, his dark eyes shining at the world with hope and trust. The resource manager leafed through the folder. There were requests for pay increases and paid vacations; notices of the man's marriage and of the births of his three daughters; occasional promotions accompanied by nagging memos that he hadn't yet got his increase. All in all, he had had an uneventful career. Marred only by a reprimand from the owner ten years before for negligently allowing an oven to be damaged by overheating, his file told the story of a hard worker who had gradually risen through the ranks. His technician's smock and oil-stained hands notwithstanding, he now earned twice as much as the human resources manager.

By now the loaf of bread looked as if it had been gnawed at by a mouse. Throwing its remains into the wastepaper basket, he put on his coat, still wet from the rain, and headed back to the bakery, now nearly invisible behind a pall of fog and chimney smoke.

9

As Tuesday was the night on which the bakery fulfilled its orders from the army, the ovens and conveyor belts were still going full-blast. He asked a cleaning woman for a smock and cap and went to warn the night shift supervisor not to talk to the journalist. It took a while to find him; he was with two technicians, the three of them peering into the empty bowels of an oven, trying to determine why it was making a screeching noise.

Once again the human resources manager felt envious of the bakery workers for having to deal only with dough and machinery. The supervisor, flushed from the heat and wearing a smock and apron, was deep in conversation with the technicians. In his aging, troubled face the resource manager could still make out the dark-eyed soldier in the Ordnance Corps who had been so full of vitality.

Their glances met. The supervisor did not seem surprised to see him. Perhaps he realized that aggressive yet scattershot investigation by the secretary had not closed the dead woman's case. The resource manager, anxious to spare him embarrassment in front of the technicians, waved a friendly hello and asked:

"Can I have a few minutes of your time?"

The supervisor threw the oven a last glance. Still concerned about the noise it was making, he ordered the technicians to bank the fires.

"Take her down a few degrees," he said.

10

Sighing with relief at the departure of the cafeteria's last diners, we finished placing the chairs on the tables before mopping encrusted red mud from the floor which resembled that of a slaughterhouse after the day's torrential rain, when the two of them entered out of the dark. Exhausted though we were by the customers who had flocked here all day to get out of the rain, how could we refuse them? One was the young personnel manager, whose secretary we knew, because it was she who arranged for us to cater the parties given for retiring staff. The other was a regular customer, the night shift supervisor. If our cafeteria was the only warm, quiet place two senior staff members could find in the entire bakery complex, far be it from us to disappoint them. We warned them, though, that the kitchen was closed and that a pot of tea was the most they could expect.

That was fine with the personnel manager. Without bothering to ask the supervisor, who looked preoccupied, he took a table by the window. We went on mopping and scrubbing while listening with one ear to their conversation in the hope of learning how long they would take.

At first the young personnel manager did the talking and the supervisor listened. Still in his overalls, covered by an old army jacket, he propped his chin on one hand. After a while the two fell silent, as if they had used up every last word. But then a response came, at first in a low, hesitant voice. And when the floor was spotless and dry and the chairs were lowered again from the tables, and the violet light of a clearing sky shone through the window, we were shocked to see the older man bury his face in his hands as if hiding something painful or shameful, as if he had finally understood why an empty cafeteria had been chosen for his confession.

Although the human resources manager began by apologizing for his secretary's rudeness, which had been inexcusable if only because of the presence of other workers, the night shift supervisor did not appear to be concentrating. Far from owing him an apology, the secretary, he seemed to believe, had been within her rights. Only when the manager described the old owner's agitation, which made it necessary to get at the truth, did the supervisor begin to focus, as if grasping at last that the problem wasn't a clerical one.

The resource manager hastened to reassure him. As important as it was to ascertain the facts, he had been through the supervisor's file and knew about his loyalty and devotion to the company. Whatever was said tonight would remain between them. He did not intend to file another reprimand, like the one the supervisor had received for the damaged oven.

The supervisor was taken aback to learn that the owner's handwritten rebuke was still on his record.

"All such documents come in duplicate. Their natural and final resting place is the filing cabinet in my office."

Gently, the resource manager explained his intentions. Having taken this unpleasant business on himself, he was determined to get to the bottom of it and report back to the owner after the concert.

"The concert?"

"Yes. Just imagine: he couldn't miss his concert! While we're running around in the wind and rain to save his reputation, he's having a musical evening. Well, why not? We all need inspiration. Who can object these days to some good music?"

In short, the younger man was proposing to cover for the older man, who outranked him by two levels and earned nearly twice as much. To do so efficiently, however, even in a trivial matter like this, he had to know the whole truth. The weasel meant to strike again. From his point of view, why shouldn't he?

"The weasel?"

The human resources manager laughed. "That journalist. It's my name for him." They had just had a nasty phone conversation and exchanged insults; frankly, even "weasel" was too kind a description. "We have to be careful. I don't want you talking to journalists, even if their questions seem perfectly innocent."

"But what does he want?"

"A personal apology from the owner. A clear admission of guilt. No mere explanation can exonerate us of what he calls our callousness. He'll keep trying to prove that that woman was still employed by us – not only at the time of her death, but afterwards too."

"What do you mean, afterwards?"

"I mean even now. He thinks of her as a damsel in distress and of himself as her knight errant. You can be sure it won't take him long to find out about your unreported termination of employment."

"I've already said I'm sorry about that. I really am. I'll pay the costs . . . "

The resource manager explained that feeling sorry and paying the costs were not the issue. The truth alone was. An unidentified female corpse still in a morgue a week after a bombing was an irresistible temptation for idealistic reporters.

"Temptation?" The supervisor was taken aback. Actually, he replied, there was a temptation in any helpless stranger – a live one, that is, not a dead one. The vulnerability of temporary or foreign workers was somehow . . .

"Tempting?" The casually uttered word had taken on a life of its own. "How so?"

"I mean . . . " The supervisor struggled to be exact. "It's not just having power over them. It's pity and sympathy too . . . you're sucked into it."

Flustered, he explained in a shaky voice that he didn't want to be misunderstood. Nor did he owe anyone an explanation. The fact was . . . well, nothing had actually happened between them. Nothing physical. Yet he had to admit that he had thought of her all the time. This was why, since running the night shift wasn't simple, he had had to ask her to leave – for her own good.

The resource manager hadn't expected such frankness. He winced as he had done when discovering the CV he had recorded. It was as if this woman ten years older than himself, whom he still couldn't remember, was threatening to become a temptation for him too.

He chose his words carefully. He had already begun to suspect, he said, that the problem was not just work-related. Even though he was tired, and anxious to join his waiting daughter, this was what had kept him on the case. He wanted to know exactly what had happened. Was there more to it than the supervisor was owning up to? His secretary had been deeply impressed by the dead woman's beauty – and that damned journalist had spoken of it, too. It was unbelievable that even there, in a hospital morgue, someone had had the cheek to . . .

"What?" The supervisor turned pale.

Not that looks were always that important, the human resources manager continued, still, it was understandable if . . . besides feeling for her loneliness . . . that is, if she really had been that attractive . . . or was this putting it too strongly? He himself, after all, despite having interviewed her personally, couldn't remember the first thing about her, not even with the aid of her photograph.

Although the drainpipes outside the window were still dripping, the storm had abated. The supervisor looked tranquil, meditative. He did not seem the least bit upset by the confession that the human resources manager was about to extract from him. The crew-cut man, twenty years younger than he was, inspired confidence.

II

And so, swallowing the last of his no longer hot tea, the supervisor gropingly told his story. The resource manager said nothing. Only once, noticing that the kitchen workers had finished setting the tables for breakfast, did he plead with a hand signal for their patience until the confession, which he did not believe would be long, was complete.

In theory, he should have been right. The man confessing was a mechanically minded fellow who had come to the bakery straight from the Ordnance Corps without continuing his education. Although he could have opened a small business of his own, he had preferred to take a low-paying job that gave him the opportunity to learn the ropes of the baking trade. From job to job and division to division, he had been promoted steadily until his appointment six years ago to night shift supervisor. This was the busiest and most important of the shifts, the only one that baked for the army, which demanded a high level of quality control . . .

The lights were going out in the cafeteria. One by one, the workers left for home. Only two, an old Jewish waiter and a young Arab dishwasher, stayed behind to lock up. The supervisor, still extracting a first thread from the tangle of his story, was candidly describing the fascination that the swan-necked cleaning woman had had for him. It was this fascination, he now understood, that had allowed him to dismiss her and keep her employed at the same time.

It certainly hadn't been her looks. As one senior staff member to another, he swore again that nothing had happened between them. It was a purely emotional matter, the exact nature of which he seemed reluctant to describe, as if that might make his guilt or sorrow grow. Their first meeting, which had also been their longest, had had to do entirely with work. It had taken place in late autumn or early winter, after the woman had been transferred, at her request, to the better-paying night shift.

The supervisor had a strict rule: no matter where new workers came from or what their previous experience had been, he personally briefed them on all safety regulations. And the cleaning crew were briefed the longest, not only because they were generally the least educated and least attentive, but also because they cleaned everywhere and everything. They had to be warned of the dangers of the ovens and the milling blades, the cantankerous dough mixers and the intricate conveyors.

It was already after midnight when he'd found time for the new recruit. Although she was familiar with the bakery from her job on the day shift, he gave her the entire tour. Had he known she was an engineer, he would undoubtedly have cut the briefing short; even then he would have insisted on a tour.

The night shift supervisor had many women working under him and was accustomed to setting boundaries that prevented complications. The new cleaning woman, who followed him obediently while listening to his instructions with a bright smile, her smock and cap making her look middle-aged and bulky, had been no exception. And yet he could sense his own reluctance to finish the briefing and send her back to her mops and brooms. This woman, even just her proximity, seemed to promise something he had always known about but never dreamed of for himself. He had lectured her on the bakery's strict hygienic standards, as he guided her through the dark, hidden corners behind the ovens (which as a rule he didn't do), and all the while he had felt a twinge of sweetness at the sight of her smile, which somehow, after it left her lips, continued to shine in her unusual Tartar, or perhaps Mongol, eyes.

"Tartar or Mongol?" The human resources manager thought this was overstating it. The tilt of her eyes, which he recalled from the computer image, was actually quite delicate and subtle.

But the supervisor, though he had never known a Tartar or a Mongol, repeated the comparison. He was now working his way deeper into his confession. What captivated him most had not been the woman's smile or even her charm, but the contradictions of a fair-complexioned Asiatic, with whom he had suddenly fallen – passively and with no hope of con-summation – in love.

The waiter, who had been waiting impatiently with his coat and boots on, came to bid them good night while assuring them that they could stay as long as they wished, since the dishwasher had decided to sleep in the cafeteria and would make them coffee to get them through the rest of the night.

"The night?" Once again the human resources manager was having whole nights thrust on him. "We don't need it. We're almost finished . . ."

And yet, like the resource manager's secretary – who after

resisting returning to the office had plunged into the case to the detriment of her home and family – the supervisor had apparently forgotten all about his shift and even about the screeching oven. What had happened to him, he wanted his younger colleague to understand, had been complicated, even dangerous. The Tartar woman had got under his skin . . .

Worse than that. Even had he sought to stamp out the flames by returning quickly to the work floor, his own employees – the technicians, the storeroom chiefs, the bakers – would have prevented it. Over the years they had learned to respect not only his wishes but his feelings, and they now conveyed to him that they were well aware of his inner state. Refraining from badgering him with the usual pressing matters, they had let him take his time with the smiling woman who walked, gently nodding, past their assembly lines. Their unspoken complicity surprised him. All he could imagine was that they desired to assist him – a sombre, domesticated man with three grandchildren – to live out a kind of infatuation that he had no longer deemed himself capable of.

The next morning, in the quiet of his bedroom, at an hour generally devoted to sleep, he had awakened with a delicious discomfort and anxious thoughts about the night ahead and his second encounter with the new employee now under his wing.

He was talking unprompted now, encouraged by the silence of the human resources manager, who realized that this story, which had seemed simple enough that afternoon in the old owner's office, was getting more involved as the night wore on. Not even the aromatic Turkish coffee brought by the Arab dishwasher could hasten its denouement. Indeed, it only prolonged it.

On the whole, the supervisor continued, he had no direct dealings with the cleaning staff, whose requests and complaints were handled by the floor foremen. In the bakery's open work space, constantly crossed by dozens of employees, there was no way to exchange even a few words with the new woman without being immediately noticed. The knowledge that he was being watched disconcerted him. Yet it was flattering that his workers cared for him not only as their superior but also as a person in his own right, however grey and ordinary. Although at first he'd thought their concern merely served as a distraction from the tedium of work, he soon realized that they hoped his falling in love would soften his hard edges, which they had learned to fear.

The resource manager stole a glance at his watch. Although the fine-featured man in the stained work garb was baring his soul with an unnecessary thoroughness, the death he was leading up to made it inadvisable to interrupt him. It still remained to be seen where the slip-up – the unterminating termination of employment – had occurred . . .

The thought, real or imaginary, that the entire night shift wished him to be in love had only made the supervisor's position even more difficult, more untenable. He knew well that his attraction to the new worker, even if its painful intensity remained unexpressed, might end tragically.

"Tragically?" The resource manager was troubled by so fraught a word. What exactly did the mechanically minded supervisor, the former Ordnance Corps soldier, mean by it?

By the second night, the supervisor went on, he was aware that he could locate the new woman by a single glance at the dozens of workers around him. And the more he tried to conceal it, the more he kept track of her movements with a second, inward glance, physical and incorporeal at once, even when he was inside an oven or bent over a mixer. He demanded nothing of her – only to know that her bright smile, which kept renewing itself for no reason as she scrubbed the burned crusts of dough from the day shift's bread pans, was still there.

Yet this, too, did not escape those workers who knew him best and cared the most for him. Nonchalantly, casually, in the early hours of the morning, when the minds of night shift workers sometimes wander, they let slip details about her. Despite her vivaciousness and charm, she was a lonely

44

woman. An elderly friend had accompanied her to Israel; then, however, disappointed at not having found a decent job, he had returned to Russia, as had her only child, an adolescent boy whose father, her ex-husband, did not want him living in a dangerous city. She alone, for some reason, had insisted on staying, which made it necessary for her to look for a new male protector . . .

The resource manager was momentarily tempted to tell the supervisor that all this information existed in his own hand-writing in the dead woman's file. It was unfortunate, he thought, that someone of the supervisor's standing was forced to depend on work floor gossip, when he could consult the file of any worker on his shift.

Or could he? Glad he had said nothing, the resource manager made a note to ask his secretary or, better still, the old owner – who was by now enjoying the opening bars of the concert and had no idea with what determination his staff was defending his humanity . . .

And that, the supervisor said, the words now tumbling out of him, was what he had been waiting for. Her radiant solitude made him want to protect it. He wasn't looking for a love affair. He was too old for that, besides being too busy and set in his ways. All he asked for was the right to serve as the new worker's invisible custodian until she could stand on her own two feet. His children were independent and no longer needed him, and his quick glances at the Russian cleaning woman told him that, as cheerful as she tried to be, life was hard for her in the depths of the night. She never joined the other workers. Leaning on her broomstick with her head on her hands, she would stand exhausted in a corner, her eternal smile playing on her lips. How pure it was, precisely because it was meant for no one! How she needed protection, and how easily he could give it to her!

It was dangerous. Of course it was. Who would guard its boundaries? Certainly not the workers on his shift, who wanted his heart to melt with a new emotion. And how did he know she wouldn't be overwhelmed? Would she be content with what he could give her and understand what he could not? It had been obvious to him from the start – unless this was just wishful thinking – that he appealed to her, although he was no longer young. She was always sweeping the floor in his vicinity, wiping the oil from machines he was working on, cleaning up after him in the men's room, tasks that were hardly required of her.

He was experienced enough to know that the night could entrap even its oldest denizens, especially in the hours before dawn, when the most nocturnal souls were prone to foolish lapses of concentration that could cause accidents and sometimes disasters. This was why, half joking and half seriously, he urged workers he encountered at that hour to take a cold drink from the fountain, splash water on their faces, or just step outside for a breath of air. It was perfectly natural for him to do this with the new employee too. Sometimes they exchanged a few words that pierced him to the quick. He tried to hide it by chatting with the other workers just as much, especially the cleaning staff.

By now he knew she sensed what was happening. It pleased her that he acted his age and was discreet, even that he had a family and grandchildren, because she wasn't looking for a new husband or boyfriend. She was resigned to the loss of both. Nor did she need another son. All she wanted, plain and simple, was a patron, someone quiet and sympathetic, and to such a man she was quite ready to grant physical favours without jeopardizing the labour of his life.

Nevertheless, since she turned up in the night shift this smiling, lonely engineer, or whatever she was, had become more dangerous than any woman who had ever worked for him, since her loneliness was an invitation not only to having fantasies but also to acting them out. Aware of how he, a man on the verge of retirement, was being encouraged to live out an impossible dream, one that was given greater legitimacy only by the desperate times the country was going through, he'd decided to dismiss the woman, but without running the risk of someone else taking her place. He'd persuaded her to leave her job and look for a better one but had kept her on the payroll, so that if she failed to find anything, or if he missed her too much, she could always return . . .

"In short" – the human resources manager broke his long silence with a single laconic sentence that contrasted starkly with the supervisor's emotional outpouring – "you thought you could make your own rules."

12

Although the two men who rose from the table had taken longer than they'd expected, they had barely made a dent in the night. The resource manager, unaware that he, too, still had a night shift ahead of him, offered the dishwasher a ride to the bus station. The young Arab, however, was happy to have the cafeteria to himself. He preferred to get a good night's sleep there without having to worry about the three humiliating checkpoints he had to pass through on the way back from his village every day.

The resource manager turned to go. Satisfied at having solved the case, he was eager to get home. Yet when the supervisor, raising the collar of his army jacket, followed him to the parking lot, he understood that the man still needed to talk. He had no choice but to say, after unlocking his car and cleaning the wet leaves from the windscreen:

"I'm sorry, but I'm in a hurry to relieve my secretary. She's looking after my daughter this evening."

The night shift supervisor, who had never imagined that so many staff members would have to be mobilized because of his falling in love, asked in distress:

"So now *she* has to know everything, too?"

"No," the resource manager said. "She doesn't and she won't. And I'll see to it that *he* won't, either." As if the old man were floating in the sky, he pointed to the spark-flecked smoke rising from the bakery's chimneys. "Your story stays with me – with the personnel division, or the human resources division, or whatever you want to call it."

47

"Well," murmured the supervisor, reluctant to part with his confessor, now a partner in his love, "if you need anyone ... I mean to identify the corpse ... I'm always available ... that is, if there's no one else ..."

The resource manager felt a slight wave of revulsion. No, he did not need anyone. The case was closed. So was the option of responding in the local weekly. "The less we dwell on this story, the better. Our biggest mistake would be to make it bigger than it is."

Arriving at his former home, he was surprised to find it so warm and brightly lit. A fresh smell of wet umbrellas and coats filled the hallway. The living room smelled of pizza. The apartment, which had been a grim place through the past year, now had an air of merry practicality. His twelve-year-old daughter sat on a pillow in a chair at the head of the large dining table, flushed and wide awake. Scattered on the table among slices of pizza, knishes, empty bottles, and coffee cups were textbooks and notebooks, a ruler, and a compass. The office manager had been as good as her word – twice as good, in fact, since her husband, whose long, flattened bald head resembled a rugby ball, was sitting beside her happily solving maths problems.

"Back so soon?" his daughter asked, with a hint of disappointment even though she was happy to see him. "We still have lots of homework to do."

For the first time since his summons to the owner's office that afternoon, he let out a laugh. "You can see which of us has the real talent for human resources," he told the office manager. "I'm sorry I'm late. The night shift supervisor wouldn't stop talking."

But the office manager was so thoroughly enjoying her new role that she was prepared to continue it. If the resource manager needed more time, she said, or wished to get to work on his response to the weekly, she and her husband were prepared to stay and help his daughter finish her homework.

"More time again!" he grumbled. "The night is over. The

case is closed. Everything is clear now. I'm just too tired to explain it all."

"Of course," the office manager agreed, slightly miffed. She would wait until the morning, when she would in any case have to type the response. Her husband was now solving the last maths problem, after which she would check the English vocabulary assignment. In the meantime, the resource manager might as well sit down and warm up. He looked cold and must be starving. There was food on the table and she would make him a hot drink. Why not be a guest in his own home?

"My ex-home," he replied with a bitter smile. Slipping out of his wet coat, he removed his damp shoes and switched on the solar heater's electrical backup for some extra hot water.

It had been agreed that in his ex-wife's absence he would spend the nights here with his daughter rather than have her come to his mother's, where he was staying until his newly rented apartment became available. Naturally, he didn't use the double bed he had been banished from; he slept on the living room couch. Two shelves in the bathroom were reserved for his toilet articles and pyjamas, with additional space for underwear, a fresh shirt, and a pair of clean trousers.

He passed his wife's darkened bedroom, which not long ago had also been his. Shutting its half-open door against the ever present temptation to peek, he locked himself in the gleaming bathroom. He had presided over its renovation just a year ago, choosing the tiles and taps and ingeniously relocating the sink and toilet, without dreaming how soon he would be brutally expelled. Yet he still regarded this room as his own. Uncertain how quickly the electricity would do the job of the sun that had hidden all day long, he took off his rumpled clothes and sat naked on the edge of the tub to test the warmth of the water.

He was still thinking about the night shift supervisor's confession. He would have to decide how much to tell the old man and how much to suppress out of respect for that clandestine and abruptly ended infatuation. It saddened him that he would never meet the woman whose identity he had

49

deciphered. A quick glance from afar was all he would have needed to get a sense of her. Like all of the company's employees – even the old man himself, who drew a monthly pay packet in addition to his dividends – she had been the responsibility of his division. What had gone through her head when she realized that although she had lost her job she was still being paid for it? Had she assumed it was the supervisor's continued declaration of love for her, or did she take it to be a clerical error that she could not afford to correct?

I'll never know . . .

And yet what does it matter?

I've already wasted enough energy on this mess.

It's time to call it a day.

The water flowing from the tap showed no sign of warming up, evidence of how little sunshine there had been that day and how slim the hope for a hot shower was. He sat shivering on the edge of the tub, naked in his former home, while the two substitute parents gave a last flurry of attention to his daughter, who was being worn down by the growing tensions between him and his ex-wife. As far as he was concerned, he thought, switching on the electric heater while gently massaging his body, they could help her with her homework as much as they liked. Perhaps before going to sleep he would find a quiet time to tell her about his evening. Hearing about the pretty woman with the smile who had spent a week in the morgue as a nameless corpse might make her realize that there were other people to feel sorry for besides herself.

There was a sharp knock on the bathroom door, followed by his daughter's strained voice:

"Abba, if you haven't showered yet, don't! Ima just called to say she's coming home because of what you got yourself into. You have to let her have her parking place. So please, Abba, if you haven't begun to shower, there's no time . . ."

He knew how she suffered from the savage rift between her parents and did not wish to make things worse for her – and so, overcoming his repugnance at having to get back into his dirty clothes, he turned off the tap and rejoined the office manager and her husband. They were already in their over-coats, holding their folded umbrellas. A khaki stocking cap, the kind worn in simpler times by Israeli soldiers, was pulled jauntily down over the husband's rugby-ball head. Here was a couple who felt good about themselves and about their contribution to the world.

"You didn't have to say goodbye," the office manager said. "You'll see me in the morning."

"But not your husband," he replied. He shook the hand of this jaunty man, who whispered a gentle scolding:

"You should have more patience with her maths. She has too many gaps in her education."

The human resources manager reddened and laid a hand on his heart. Then, slipping into his windcheater, he accompanied the two to the street. When, he asked the office manager, did she think the concert would be over?

"You don't intend to call him tonight!"

"Why not? After all the fuss he's made, he deserves some kind of report."

"And you've really cleared everything up?"

"I think so."

She regarded him sympathetically. "In that case, you can call until midnight. Don't worry if he sounds half asleep. He dozes off and wakes up all the time. He'll sleep better tonight if you calm him."

"I'm not sure I will," said the resource manager. He parted from them warmly, as if they were newly discovered relatives; moved his car from the building's parking lot to the far pavement; and returned to the apartment, where he devoured the remains of the pizza and told his daughter the story of the cleaning woman. He even showed her the woman's photograph in the folder, curious to see how it struck her. Yet she did not seem to have an opinion or even to be listening. Gripping his arm, she pleaded:

"Abba! Ima will be here any minute. You're both tired. Why fight again now?"

"Who says we're going to fight?"

She bit her lip and said nothing, while he stroked her curly head to still her fears. In his heart, he cursed the old owner for spoiling their evening. Slipping back into his damp wind-cheater, he borrowed an umbrella and went out into the rain. Standing in the dark entrance of the house next door, he waited to make sure that his wife arrived.

The rain was now a fine drizzle. You couldn't tell whether it was falling or rising, or whether the strange red glow in the sky, appearing behind a large antenna, was natural or man-made. Shivering from cold and fatigue, he stood waiting patiently for the large car that was still registered in his name to swing into the street and pull violently into the vacated parking space. Its driver, apparently unconvinced that the man she hated had departed, left the headlights beaming and stepped out to glance at the apartment, as if to judge from the glow in the windows, or perhaps some other sign, whether he was still there. They hadn't met face-to-face for weeks. From her silhouette he could tell that despite the weather she was wearing high heels. No doubt she had on an elegant dress beneath her winter coat. And yet, he thought sadly, finding a new man wasn't easy for her. Whoever she had gone out of town to meet that day must have left her feeling disappointed.

Well, that wasn't his problem.

He needn't feel guilt for her bottomless anger.

Or for her sexual frustration . . .

Assured at last that he had left, she switched off the car lights and took out a small suitcase. Then, before pressing the remote control, she glanced up once more.

Even though there were only a few metres between them, she did not notice him standing in the darkness. Yet had she sniffed a familiar scent? Whatever it was, she suddenly stopped and looked suspiciously around before hurrying up the stairs.

13

Although it was only nine o'clock, the human resources manager assumed that his mother, who was not expecting him that night, would already have gone to bed. He had noticed that she was sleeping a great deal lately, and since she claimed that her first hours of sleep were her best, he was determined to enter quietly and not disturb her. He had forgotten, however, that in his absence she always put the chain on the door. Locked out, he had to call her on his cell phone and explain what he was doing there.

She was in no hurry to let him in. As if he were a lodger rather than her only son, she slowly put on a robe and paused to comb her hair before unchaining the door with painstaking reluctance. He had turned her apartment into a transit camp, burdening her not only with his clutter but also with his divorce, which she had done all she could to prevent. For the first time since his childhood, she did not look at him when they spoke.

Now she took his unexpected arrival as evidence that he had caused yet another family mishap. Instead of helping to put his supper on the table, she went to her bedroom, gathered the still-warm sections of the day's newspaper from her sheets and blankets, dumped them on the kitchen table for him, and excused herself to return to her interrupted sleep.

He felt almost insulted. What was the hurry? he asked. The night was young. And he had a story to tell her, something from the office that he wanted to discuss, something on which he would like to have her opinion.

She had no choice but to listen to the tale about the cleaning woman, whose death in the latest bombing had led to a vicious article being scheduled in the local weekly where his photograph was to appear as well as mention of his divorce. It couldn't be stopped. That's what the press was like these days: it always went for the jugular. And yet, he said with a smile, proudly relating his discovery of the supervisor's strange infatuation, he had already managed to get to the bottom of it. Placing the folder on the table, he showed his mother the picture and asked whether she, too, found the woman alluring or attractive.

She listened to him absentmindedly, her eyes on the table, as if doubting whether anything in his account could possibly justify the loss of her beauty sleep. Nor did she want to look at the picture. "What difference does it make?" she asked crossly.

"But it does!" There had been an emotional entanglement. Why not try to understand whether it had to do with real beauty or the mere illusion of it? He himself, for example, though he had interviewed the woman for her job, had not been impressed.

"You interviewed her?"

"Of course. Every new employee has to be vetted by the human resources division."

"But if you weren't impressed by her, what does my opinion matter?"

"I didn't say it did. I'm just curious. Why are you so stubborn? How much trouble is it to look at a photograph?"

His mother made no reply. Her divorced son's fascination with the picture of a dead woman struck her as unnecessarily morbid. Since it seemed important to him, however, she asked him to fetch her glasses and cigarettes and cautiously opened the folder. She first read the newspaper article, then turned to the résumé in her son's handwriting, passed from that to the computer printout, and glanced briefly at the face of the blonde woman. She lit a cigarette, inhaled, and asked how old the woman had been.

"I can tell you exactly. Forty-eight."

"Have you told the morgue what you know?"

"Not yet."

"Why not?"

"Right now it's for internal use. We have to decide how to formulate our response. Until we do I'm keeping it under wraps."

"Under wraps?" His mother gave a start. "From whom?"

"From that vile journalist who plans to write another instalment, for one."

"But the morgue needs to know who she is. Why not tell them?"

"It's only for a day or two. Even then, I'll talk only to authorized parties. And before I do, I'll need to double-check my sources. The last thing we want is an exposé of the supervisor's private life. With weasels like that journalist, you have to watch out ... By the way, the owner doesn't know a thing yet. He went to a concert and let me run myself ragged."

His mother, enveloped in cigarette smoke, did not like his procrastination one bit. Surely the dead woman must have friends or family who were looking for her.

"I don't believe anyone is looking for her. But to be honest, who knows?"

He brought her an ashtray.

"Not you, that's for sure." There was disdain, even anger, in her voice. "I'm warning you, though. Once you've discovered who she is, she's yours."

"How come?"

"She's your responsibility. Keeping it to yourself is not only disrespectful, it's criminal. Tell me" – she was raising her voice now as if he were once again a small boy – "what's your problem? Why can't you phone the hospital? What are you afraid of?"

He removed the dishes from the table, scraping the waste into the bin, placed them in the sink, and rinsed them. "It's the middle of the night," he said gently. "A morgue isn't an emergency room. No one is sitting there waiting to hear from me. Divulging details over the telephone that can end up in the wrong place is worse than doing nothing. If she's been lying unidentified for a week, she can wait one more night. Believe me, her ordeal is over."

His mother said nothing. She took off her glasses, stubbed out her cigarette, reached for the review section of the news-paper, and headed for her bedroom. Going into the bathroom to check the water, he discovered it was cold here, too. Well, his mother had not known he was coming. He switched on the old boiler, put some water on for tea, and glanced at the front section of the newspaper. Then, before his mother could turn her light out, he went to ask for the sports section. Had she already thrown it away? He addressed her timidly; even now, their eyes did not make contact.

"You must think something. I mean about that picture."

She preferred not to answer. "It's hard to say. It's so small . . ."

"Even so."

She hesitated, weighing her words. "Your boss's office manager may be right. There's something about her . . . especially the eyes . . . or maybe it's her smile. It's like sunshine."

A wave of chagrin swept over him. For some reason, it grieved him to be told that the woman was beautiful. His mother, who seemed to know this without looking at him, tried retracting her remark, then gave up.

"Should I leave the light on for you in the hallway?"

"Why? Are you going out again tonight?"

"Yes. There's no hot water for a shower."

"How was I supposed to know you were coming?"

"You weren't. I'm not blaming you." He shifted his weight to his other leg. "While the water is heating, I'll run over to the morgue. Maybe I can find someone there to take her off my hands."

"At this hour?" She sat up in bed. "Don't you think it's rather late?"

"Not really. It's just a little after nine."

"What hospital is she in?"

"Mount Scopus."

"There's a morgue there?"

"You're asking me? So I've been told . . ."

She was beginning to feel sorry for him.

"Perhaps you're right about putting it off until tomorrow. That wouldn't be so terrible."

"*Now* you tell me that?" he snapped. "After first making me feel all that guilt?"

He turned out the light.

14

Sometime before 10 p.m. he appeared at our security hut, a stocky man with a hard, weary face. Although the storm had subsided, in his winter overcoat, galoshes, gloves, and yellow woollen scarf he seemed prepared for more bad weather. And yet he was bareheaded. Before he could say a word, we searched him for guns and explosives. "You want the morgue? At this hour?" He said he was looking for our director, assuming there was such a person.

That gave us a fright. Had there been a new bombing we didn't know about? But no, he had come, so it seemed, in connection with last week's bombing, which no one remembered any more. He waved a thin folder and said that he had discovered the identity of a woman killed in that bombing.

"We're sorry, sir," we answered, "but it's after visiting hours. You need special permission to be admitted at night." Yet after he showed us his ID card and told us he managed the personnel department of a bakery that supplied half the country with bread, we said, "More power to someone like you, who with hundreds of people working under him, still comes to ask about a temporary cleaning woman – a dead one, in fact." He liked that. Then he asked again how to get to the morgue.

How could we tell a personnel manager where it was when we ourselves, in all our years of working here, had never been there? We had to call the emergency room and ask for directions.

Although the directions did not seem complicated, he was soon wandering up and down hallways and stopping interns and nurses, who had only the vaguest idea of where the dead were kept. Finally, hoping to find someone who was better informed, he went to the main office. The woman at the desk already knew about him. Not being authorized to receive his report, however, she drew him a map to help him reach the morgue and promised that somebody would be there to receive him.

The map did not, as he had imagined it would, instruct him to descend to the ground floor and look there for stairs to a hidden basement. Rather, it guided him outside to a small cluster of pine trees in which stood an old, stone building, one wing of which, according to a sign, was a stockroom for medical supplies. A second wing housed the department of forensic medicine, while a third, unidentified, was no doubt the one he was looking for. He had to stumble down a dark lane to reach it. Twinkling lights in the distance, which came not from stars but from far-off houses, hinted at a panoramic view by day.

It was remarkable, reflected the human resources manager, who did not consider himself easily frightened, that no effort had been made to conceal the place. On the contrary: it stood in the open by the pine trees, untended and unguarded, as though it were just another office you could walk into and out of without fearing the dead any more than they feared you. Although a light was shining in a small window, he wasn't sure anyone was there. What will be, will be, he told himself. At least now I'm dressed for the weather. Even if I'm on a wild-goose chase, it will save me time tomorrow. Meanwhile, the water is heating in the boiler and I'll be rid of the real or unreal guilt my mother is trying to pin on me.

He knocked on the locked door. No answer. Circling the building, he came to a back door that opened when he pushed it. Without warning, he found himself in a cold, dimly lit space; an air conditioner was humming softly. A dozen or so stretchers with corpses on them were arranged in two parallel lines. Some of the bodies were well wrapped. Others, apparently intended for research or the classroom, were covered with transparent sheets of plastic.

The human resources manager froze. With all due respect for the rational belief that death was the end of all things, it was irresponsible to leave the door unlocked. Suppose he were unbalanced or given to morbid fantasies? He could easily panic and file a lawsuit.

Standing still, he shut his eyes, took a deep breath, and prayed that there would be no bad or strange smell. Allowing himself a furtive glance, very much like his mother's in recent months, he noticed a corpse the colour of yellow clay. The plastic sheet that enveloped it was too thick for him to tell if the body was a man's or a woman's. Even though he felt sufficiently composed to examine the stretchers for the cleaning woman's identifying tag, his uninvited presence in the room struck him as a breach of etiquette. Reluctantly, he backed out, then shut the door with a click.

And yet, nevertheless ... *I've made it to the last stop*, he thought. *I was here. It's not my job to identify a woman I don't know. I've come to report, not to investigate. Tomorrow I'll wrap things up with a telephone call. If the worse comes to the worst, I'll come back. It's not something I can ask the old man or my secretary to do, let alone the night shift supervisor, who might be tempted to take too passionate a farewell look. He's in no state for it. I promised to spare him a reprimand, not to arrange a last rendezvous with his beloved – who, legally, until the authorities find her next-of-kin, is still my or my division's responsibility.*

In his mind's eye he was transported to the vast work floor of the bakery, with its rattling production lines twisting in doughy arabesques. Although this dough after reaching the ovens would become tomorrow's bread, its yellow-clay colour bore an eerie resemblance to that of the corpse he had just seen.

He circled the building, wondering how far it was to the distant lights. Snug in his layers of clothing, he felt ready for any adventure. But the lights had vanished in a dark mist. The night, which had seemed about to clear, now grew so dense that the smock of an approaching lab technician looked like the flapping wings of an angel.

15

The woman at the office had kept her word and found someone at the pathology lab who knew the ins and outs of the morgue.

He was a stout man of about fifty, wearing a French beret that could have been a token of bohemianism, a kind of Orthodox skullcap, or both. Full of curiosity and energy, he hailed the resource manager standing in the darkness with a barrage of words. "It's good you came tonight, because she would have been gone by tomorrow. You would have had to chase after her to the Central Pathology Institute, where all the unsolved cases are sent. The doctors and nurses from intensive care managed to keep her body here until now because they were hoping that a friend, relative, or fellow worker of hers would turn up. They wanted someone to know how hard they had fought to save her life and why they couldn't. We're a small hospital here, far from the centre of town, and we don't generally get the critical or even the severe cases. Perhaps the police and emergency teams don't think we're well enough equipped. Still, it's a blow to our professional pride. I suppose she was brought here because she didn't seem in serious condition at first, even though she was unconscious. The only visible damage was a few small puncture wounds in her hands and feet and a scratch on her skull. These certainly didn't look fatal. Only afterwards did it turn out that she had an infection of the brain, perhaps from a bacterial source in the market."

"The brain?" said the manager wonderingly. "I didn't know it could get infected, too."

"Of course it can. Why not? She lay for two days until nothing more could be done. She was so silent and anonymous that everyone was touched by her. The staff did all they could. They wanted so badly for her to regain consciousness, if only to find out who she was. That's why she was kept in the morgue longer than usual. We hoped there would be someone to hear how we had tried ... that she wouldn't just be forgotten. It's your luck you didn't wait until morning. Even if you're only a personnel manager, we're counting on you for an identifying clue. Let's first go to the office and fill out a National Insurance form. No one understood why her place of work didn't come looking for her."

The stout lab technician pulled out a key ring and unlocked the front room of the morgue. Although the human resources manager considered saying something about the open back door, he refrained. *Let's see what this fellow has to tell me*, he thought. Affably offering him a seat by a stretcher, the technician took out a tattered blue shopping bag from a metal cabinet. Attached to it was a manila envelope with the cleaning woman's death certificate, a medical report, and the torn, bloodstained pay slip. The technician, who had no doubt been through its contents before, turned it over and shook out two yellow keys tied with a string.

"That's it," he declared. "Apart from a few rotten cheeses and vegetables, which we couldn't keep because of the smell. Let's get what you know about her down on paper. I hope" – he smiled pleasantly – "that you're not too squeamish to identify her. If you're worried about it, let me assure you that you're fortunate. She's in perfect condition. Believe me, she looks like a sleeping angel."

The resource manager turned red and gave the technician, who looked pleased with his metaphor, a hostile glance. He felt sure that this was the "inside source" who had tipped off the newspapers. It's all because of him, he thought, that I'm still on the job at this hour. Coldly, he set him straight. He wasn't squeamish in the least. He was quite capable of looking reality in the face, no matter how ugly it was – provided it needed to be looked at. But he was only here to supply the dead woman's name, address, and ID number, all traced from the pay slip – the existence of which had been irresponsibly divulged to an unreliable journalist instead of being passed on to him, the company's personnel manager. Although he had to his surprise discovered that he had interviewed the woman and even taken down her CV, this didn't qualify him to identify her corpse. The company employed three shifts with 270 or 280 employees – 300, if you included the management. Was he supposed to recognize each one of them?

Opening the top button of his overcoat, the resource manager took out the folder, extracted the computerized image, and laid both on an empty stretcher. "Here. All that we know is in this folder. Sleeping angel or not, I have no intention of looking at her. If you think you're authorized, you do it. Here's a photograph to help you."

The lab technician, flustered, studied the image. "It's awfully small and blurry," he grumbled. "But yes, it does look like her. What was her name, Yulia? Well, it all adds up. We thought we might be dealing with a foreigner. Could she really have been forty-eight? We took her to be younger ... but yes, it's definitely her. Look at the Asiatic tilt of the eyes ... was she a Tartar? Where was she from? Believe me, the doctors and nurses in intensive care were smitten by her, even though she was unconscious ... It's her for sure. Look, why stand on ceremony? Who's going to challenge your signature? Let's have a quick look at her and get it over with. If you ask me, she'd like to leave this place too. Just sign the form and National Insurance will track down her next-of-kin so that we can get her ready for the funeral, whether it's here or overseas."

"Why don't you sign?"

"I'm not allowed to. An identification by a hospital staff member having no previous acquaintance with the deceased is inadmissible. It would only get me into trouble. I'm not even supposed to have looked at her. But you're a different case. She worked for you. If you came all the way out here on a night like this, what's stopping you now? If you don't sign, we'll have to find an employee of yours to do it, and by then she'll be at Central Path. That means a whole new bureaucratic procedure ... maybe more newspaper articles too."

The resource manager reacted sharply. "Newspapers? I thought so!"

"What's wrong with them?" The lab technician smiled shrewdly. "The dead make good copy. We've already had one journalist here ... how else would you have heard about it?"

This was going too far. "You might at least admit that you yourself were the source. Leaking private information about the dead ... don't tell me that's legal!"

The technician was unfazed. "Nothing is illegal when there isn't any choice. The only hope of identifying her was by

62

publicizing her case. But I swear I had nothing to do with the article itself. That was entirely the reporter's doing. I heard you called him a weasel. Did you actually do that to his face?"

"I did not. Where did you get that from?"

"Well, perhaps you told the weekly's secretary and she passed it on. Don't be upset. 'Weasel' is too good for him. If I know him, he took it as a compliment. It's all water off a duck's back. Weasel, eh? Not bad! But the useful kind. He's neither dumb nor lazy."

"Damn it! When did you last talk to him?"

"Right after you did. An hour or an hour and a half ago. That's why I'm working overtime. I was expecting you."

"You were?"

"Does it surprise you that we'd like to be rid of her as much as you would? Don't think that just because we're used to corpses we enjoy having her stay on here ... Well, what do you say? Why not sign for her? Here's the form."

The technician's garrulousness, however, only strengthened the resource manager's resolve. All that was missing was another article, one accusing him of identifying a woman he didn't remember.

He made another effort to explain himself. Death didn't frighten him. Just a few minutes ago, because of a carelessly open door, he had walked into the morgue and stayed calm despite the shock. But sign an official form? Absolutely not! What right did he have to do so?

Aware that he was causing a problem, he wondered at himself. After all, what difference did it make? Everything was perfectly clear. Whom was he punishing? The night shift supervisor? The journalist? The man facing him, who had got him into this predicament? What harm would it do to look at the woman's face? Was he afraid that he, too, would be smitten? As if he could fall in love with a corpse ...

He cautiously reached for the keys and asked if they were definitely hers. The technician shrugged. "In the pandemonium after a bombing, you never know. But they were found in her bag, next to the pay slip, so who else's could they be? All the other dead have been identified. No missing keys were reported ..."

The resource manager nodded and glanced around. Only now did he notice that the room had no windows. The ceiling was high, the kind that made you feel there was too much space above you. A naked, high-wattage bulb shed a cold light. *They must need a tall ladder to change it when it burns out*, he thought. With a slight smile he turned to the technician. "Why insist on a visual identification? We know her address. We can go to her apartment and see if the keys fit. That's indirect proof, but it's worth more than the foibles of memory."

The technician's eyes gleamed. "And if they do fit?"

"Then I'll sign the form as if I had done a visual."

The man took off his beret and tossed it excitedly onto the empty stretcher. Bohemian or Orthodox, he was quite bald.

"Excellent. But who'll go there?"

"I will," the resource manager surprised himself by saying softly, as if in a dream.

"You?"

"Yes, me. On condition that you don't inform the press you think so highly of ... What time is it? Not even ten. The address isn't far from here and should be easy to find. I know my way about Jerusalem. She's our responsibility until she's buried, and if nobody else wants to take it on themselves, then we – I mean the company management – have to do it. Perhaps we even have some insurance or compensation fund for dependents like her son ... because she does have a son, or at least she said so. If you don't mind, then, I'll sign for the keys. You can see that I'm doing my duty – and you can report that to the weasel on my behalf. And just so you don't think I'm scared of corpses, I'll allow myself another look at ... the back room. I'll be happy to have you as my guide. You can even explain why nothing smells. That would be good of you."

16

The lab technician was only too pleased to open the inner door. He turned on the light in the refrigerated room, dimly illuminating the dozen stretchers the human resources manager had seen before. Each had a corpse on it. The manager shivered, from excitement or cold. His first question was more philosophical than anatomical. At what point, he wanted to know, did a dead body become a corpse? Was it a matter of science or simply of semantics?

The lab technician was startled by the question. Such a conundrum had never occurred to him. After a moment's thought, he answered categorically: "It's a matter of time. There are exceptions, though."

"Such as?"

"Such as battlefield casualties. Time passes more quickly then. It's condensed."

He removed the plastic sheet from a stretcher, revealing a woman's brownish corpse and featureless face.

"I take it these are being kept for anatomy lessons," the human resources manager said, to reassure himself. Stepping up to the stretcher, he took a long, hard look, to show his guide, but most of all himself, how undaunted he was.

"Exactly."

"They won't be used for research?"

"No."

"And now do tell me" – the question kept nagging him – "why isn't there any smell here? That's the worst part of death, far worse than how it looks . . . "

"Actually," the technician said, with a slight smile, "there is a smell. You just don't notice it because it's so faint. But it does rub off on whoever spends enough time here. You can literally sniff such people out."

"Still," the manager begged to know – as if it were a life-and-death matter – "how do you neutralize it?"

"Do you want to know the chemical formula?"

"If it's not too complicated . . . "

"Complicated? Not especially."

The technician ticked off the mixture of alcohol, formalin, phenol, and distilled water with which the bodies were injected, four hours after death, after their natural fluids had been drained from them. It was simple and efficient.

The resource manager debated whether to call it a night or to continue his tour. Deciding to press on, he circled the room with small, museum-sized steps. Each stretcher had a number. For some reason, the swaddled corpses repelled him more than did the plastic-sheeted ones. Casting a last, impersonal look at them, he prepared to depart with a final question. How long had they been lying in this place?

"A year, at most."

"A year?"

"That's the longest you're allowed to keep a corpse. After that it has to be buried."

"That's the maximum?"

"According to the law."

"Interesting ... very interesting. Suppose you show me your oldest corpse. I'd like to see its state of preservation."

The technician led him down the row of stretchers, from one of which the plastic sheet had fallen of its own accord. The shrivelled but still bearded human figure beneath it was ancient-looking. Its features were distinct. The ecstatically shut eyes still revealed the passionate struggle with death that had taken place nearly a year before. Long forgotten by his survivors, the agony of this struggle lived on in the dead man. A shiver ran down the sturdy manager's spine. Sticking his gloved hands deep into the pockets of his overcoat, he mused:

"There's no question about it. A visit here is a must. It gives you a sense of what's important."

The lab technician nodded. "And of what isn't," he added.

The resource manager noted that the shrivelled man's skin was the colour of yellowed parchment. It almost looked like the pages of a sacred book.

"Interesting," he murmured again. "All of this is so very interesting ... "

With a glance at the technician, who seemed pleased with him, he asked if he was a believing Jew. No, the man replied. Yet there were times when anyone working here had to believe in something. Otherwise you could lose your humanity, watching so much life drain away.

A large clock ticked on the wall. After a visit like this, the manager thought, no one could accuse him of being finicky. He turned to go, then asked weakly which stretcher the cleaning woman was on. "You know," he added, for no apparent reason, "she was a mechanical engineer."

"She isn't on any of them. She's in the deep-freeze room. Are you sure you won't reconsider?" the technician asked.

The resource manager was sure. He could never pretend to identify a person he had only met in passing.

17

In the heated car, skimming the wet, empty streets of Arab Jerusalem, where streetlights were dimmer than in the Jewish half of the city, he again felt an urge to report back to the owner. Although not sure whether the concert was over, he dialled the old man's home over the car's speakerphone. The housekeeper told him in cultured, vaguely accented English that the master had not yet returned. The concert would be ending late because of an unusually long symphony in its second half.

"Probably something of Mahler's," said the resource manager, who prided himself on his musical knowledge.

The housekeeper, however, was not interested in composers, only in the length of their compositions. It was enough to know that the old man would not be home before midnight. If the resource manager wished to leave a message, she would take it down.

The resource manager decided not to. Why let the old man sleep in peace by telling him the job was done?

Crossing the invisible, yet ineradicable, line between the two halves of the city, he switched on the radio to listen to the concert. No, it wasn't Mahler. Yet it did seem to anticipate him. The oboe and clarinet were almost Mahleresque. A sudden rhythmic tattoo of repeating notes inspired him to conduct the music with one hand as he sped through the neighbourhood of Talbieh. He passed his mother's building and turned a corner by his old high school. Whose symphony was it? He might figure it out if only he could go on listening. Yet Jerusalem was too small a city to fit a whole symphony into, and he was already nearing the market that had been the scene of the bombing. Usha Street, where the dead woman had lived, was down the hill ahead of him. Rather than risk getting trapped in a maze of one-way streets and dead ends, he switched off the music, and parked on a main road. Then he detached his cell phone from its speaker and put it in the pocket of his overcoat.

When we heard the knock on the door we were already in our nightgowns, all except Big Sister, who was still wearing a dress. Although our parents had warned us before they set out for the rabbi's wedding that we must never open the door after nine o'clock for anyone, not even our own grandma, we were so excited that we ran to see who it was. We were sure it was Grandma come to watch over us in our sleep. We didn't even ask, 'Is that you, Grandma? Have you come for the night?' but opened the door right away. We almost fainted. A stranger was there, not even a religious Jew, a big strong man with short hair like our mother's when she takes off her wig before going to bed. He asked if we knew where Yulia Ragayev lived, because he had looked for her everywhere, upstairs and down, and couldn't find her. And though we should have shut the door and put on the chain and talked through the crack the way our father taught us, we all answered in a chorus: "She doesn't live here anymore, not upstairs and not downstairs. She's moved to the backyard, to the shack that was our neighbour's storeroom." Big Sister, who doesn't like us to answer in her place, hushed us and said, "She's not there now, because she works night shifts in a bakery. Sometimes she brings us a sweet challah for the Sabbath," and Middle Sister, who knows everything, began to yell, "That's not so, that's not so, don't listen to her! Yulia was fired, and Father

68

thinks she must have left Jerusalem, because he's been looking for her high and low."

The stranger smiled and explained in a soft voice that he was the manager of the bakery and that Yulia hadn't been fired. Did we remember the bombing in the market a week ago? She had been badly injured in it, and now she was in hospital, and he'd come with her keys to get something for her. He jangled them in the air for us to see.

We couldn't control ourselves any longer. Every child in the building knew Yulia. She was a nice, quiet woman, even if she wasn't religious, and we all screamed, "Oh, no, O God, what happened? What hospital is she in?" We were sure our parents would want to visit her, because it's a commandment in the Torah.

But the stranger lifted a hand and said, "Easy does it, girls. She's very ill and can't be visited right now. Just tell me: Has anyone been looking for her?"

"No," we all said. "No one. We'd have seen anyone who came." He nodded and asked where the light switch was and how to get to the yard. We had so forgotten about being careful that Big Sister jumped up and said, "Come on, I'll take you there. I'll show you every-thing." And to us she said, "That's enough, girls. Now go to bed."

But how could we go to bed when Big Sister was out in the yard with a stranger who wasn't religious? And so all five of us, Little Three-Year-Old Sister, too, ran into the cold in our flannel nighties to be with them. It was pitch black and there was mud and puddles everywhere between the old boards and old tools. We ducked beneath the laundry lines and showed the man the shack. Yulia's old nameplate had been ripped away by the storm and only the new one was left, the one with the Hebrew name we had given her, because we took it from the Bible and put it on her door, and she just smiled and let us do it.

18

The human resources manager watched the first key turn in the lock and felt certain the second would open something too. It's mission accomplished, he thought. I've got the right woman. And she's still ours, the personnel division's. But why are these sweet little girls still standing around me, shivering in their long nighties? One of them must be my daughter's age. What do they want from me? Now that I've opened the door, they must be waiting for me to go and look for what I promised to take to the hospital.

He beamed at them and said:

"Darlings, thank you for your help. It's awfully wet and cold out here. And very late, too. Run along now and go to bed before you catch cold."

Although all six sisters, from the biggest to the smallest, were startled by his strict, if fatherly, tone, they wavered for a moment, as if unsure whether an irreligious stranger need be obeyed. Then, all at once, like a flock of birds warned of danger by a single wing flap, they flew off without looking back. Stepping into the shack, he entered a cool, dark space whose smell of ancient sleep seemed never to have been aired.

He switched on the overhead light. The bulb was weak and he had trouble seeing even after lighting a small table lamp. The bed was rumpled, as if a bad dream had made the sleeper jump out on the last morning she had risen. Behind the pillow was another lamp, attached to the wall. Now there was enough light to survey the room.

For a second, he recoiled. Who had given him permission to be here? Yet he quickly collected himself. The company's humanity was under attack; it was time for compassion, concern, and involvement, not apologies. If he were to dispose of this woman's belongings and try to arrange compensation, he had to find a human link to her. Yes, compensation. Why not?

A doll in the form of a barefoot monk lay at the foot of the bed. It had a black robe and a beard of flax, dyed black, on its face. The resource manager held it up to see what it was made of before placing it on a shelf beside a small transistor radio, which he could not resist turning on, hoping to catch the end of the concert. Removing his gloves, he fiddled with the stations. For a while, there was a confusion of sounds; then he

70

found the wavelength of the unknown, sonorous symphony; the wind section was now trumpeting a solemn slow movement. Carefully holding the little radio, he removed, with a twinge of emotion, a flowery blouse from a wobbly straw armchair, sat down, and shut his eyes.

Back in his days as a salesman, when he'd spent many a night in hotels and lived in constant fear of insomnia, he had made a point of never going to bed before midnight. Now, after leaving his wife and moving in with his mother, he had developed the habit of taking a short but sound nap every evening, when the TV news came on. This helped him stay fresh for a night of bar hopping in the smart new establishments in town, where he hoped to meet someone new. Tonight, though, the nap would have to be symbolic, hastily snatched in the room of the departed cleaning woman.

Although both the door and the main window were shut tight, it was bitingly cold in the shack even with his coat and scarf on. The reason, he saw when he went to look for it, was another, small, open window in the bathroom. A laundry line ran from it to a nearby fence. Visible in the light of the cloud-stalked moon, clothing flapped lightly in the breeze.

If he couldn't find some friend or relative to take possession of this woman's disrupted domesticity, the resource manager thought, he would have to ask his secretary to do it. He was sure she would welcome any task that took her away from the routine of her computer. Meanwhile, he decided, he would at least close the window. He put his gloves back on and – after ascertaining that the symphony would not be ending for a while – went out into the yard. Going to the rear of the little shack, which suggested a fairy-tale hut in its wintry setting of old boards and implements, he detached the laundry line from the fence and gently gathered the rain-drenched, mud-and-leaf-spattered articles, which felt light and intimate to the touch. Back inside, he put them in the sink, wondered briefly whether he had the right to rinse them, then turned on the tap, which surprised him by running hot at once. The neighbour whose storeroom this had been had connected its

71

plumbing to his own. Wouldn't the night shift supervisor love to be here! But he mustn't have anything to do with this. His infatuation had caused enough problems.

The music on the other side of the thin bathroom wall was showing the first signs of resolution. He shut the tap and left the laundry in the sink, already regretting having taken it from the line. He mustn't touch anything else: no drawers, no documents, no photographs. Suppose the sought-for friend or relative were to turn up and accuse him of theft? What would he say? "Where have you been?" "Why didn't you take any interest in her until now?"

He sat down again in the chair, one ear on the symphony that was now slowly but surely winding down, and surveyed the dead woman's domain. Apart from the bed, which she had perhaps intended to return to that fateful morning, everything was neatly arranged. Though poor, she had had good taste. A clean plate lay on the table beside a folded napkin, mute testimony to a never-eaten last meal. Two anemones stood in a thin vase, still fresh-looking although the water had evaporated.

The walls were bare except for a single, unframed sketch. There were no photographs – none of the son whisked away by his father; none of the boyfriend who had left her; none even, of the old mother in the village who had hoped to join her. The sketch, done by an amateur – herself? – in charcoal, depicted a small, deserted alleyway – in Jerusalem's Old City? – that curved gently to meet the silhouette of a domed and minareted mosque.

The solemn music had become trapped in a frightful dissonance from which it was struggling to escape. As the little radio, in turn, struggled to transmit this, he guessed the composer in a flash. There's no doubt of it, he thought, conducting with one arm. Who but that stubborn, pious old German would ever be so tedious?

He was pleased at having figured it out. When he phoned the old man, he would surprise him not only with his detective work but also with a discussion of the concert.

"Believe it or not, I listened to it while on the job. I just couldn't tell if it was the Seventh or the Eighth."

Something about the shack, tucked away in a backyard in a semi-Orthodox neighbourhood in the centre of town, appealed to him. He wondered how much rent its owner had got away with charging. "Yulia Ragayev, Yulia Ragayev," he declaimed to the empty room. "Yulia Ragayev, Yulia Ragayev." The death of this beautiful woman a few years his senior, who had passed so close to him without his having noticed her magical smile, saddened him greatly.

The dark, earnest notes of the German symphony, which had reached its final coda, were interrupted by the jingly melody of his cell phone. Fortunately, the caller had patience, since it wasn't easy to find the tiny instrument in the many pockets of his overcoat. "Hang on," he shouted as he turned down the music. Yet when he returned to the phone, it was only his mother. Unable to sleep, she was calling to ask if he had been to the hospital and found someone to deal with the dead woman.

"Yes," he replied with a sigh. "I was in the morgue on Mount Scopus. On top of everything, they wanted me to look at the corpse."

"And you agreed?" she asked in consternation.

"Of course not. I'm not that naïve. You tell me: how can I identify someone I don't remember?"

For once, she was pleased with him. "You were right to put your foot down. It's none of your business. At last you showed some sense. Where are you, in a bar?"

He debated whether to tell her, then did.

"At her place? Why?"

He explained as briefly as possible.

"And you were able to open the door?"

"Of course."

"What did you hope to find there?"

"Nothing. I'm just having a look around. I've been thinking. Maybe the company should be a bit more generous. Someone has to pay for shipping her belongings to her family ..."

"Be careful. Don't touch anything."

"Why would I touch anything? What's there to touch? Hang on a minute, mother, hang on . . . "

The final bars of the symphony seemed to have taken the audience by surprise. The polite, weary applause from the transistor sounded at first like an idling engine. Only gradually, as if the listeners wished to spare the musicians' feelings, did it pick up. The resource manager hoped that the concert had not exhausted the old man. He wanted to give him a full report tonight. Cautiously he turned up the volume, waiting for the name of the work to be announced. Yet all he heard was the applause, still rising and falling softly. Although a kind soul tried cheering the orchestra, or perhaps himself, with a long cry of "Bravo," his remained a voice in the wilderness. It was late, and everyone wanted to go home.

"Just a minute, mother . . . hang on . . . " He reluctantly returned to the phone before she could get too indignant.

"What's wrong? Is anyone with you?"

"No. Who could be with me? I was just waiting to hear the name of a symphony played on the radio."

"Is there anything else you want from me?"

"Anything *I* want from *you*?" He was startled. "Not that I can think of."

"Well, then, good night."

"I won't be late."

"You'll come when you come."

Before his hunch could be confirmed, the musical broadcast was interrupted by the hourly news. The human resources manager switched off the radio.

The rain was beating down again on the roof of the shack. He was tired. *Still*, he thought to brace himself, *if I've gone to such lengths not to disappoint the old man, I can't let him down now. His car and driver are waiting for him at the concert hall, and he'll be home soon. If I were a bit kinkier, I might be tempted to take a nap in this bed and cover myself with the blanket. But I am who I am. I'm not a lover, or in love, or a beloved. I'll just fold the blanket neatly and move on.*

74

19

Half an hour later, he phoned the owner and found him at home. "After Bruckner's Eighth," he inquired, "are you up to listening to me?"

"Why the Eighth?" the old man marvelled. "It was the Ninth."

"Ah," the manager said, hastening to correct himself while displaying his knowledge. "The unfinished one."

"Unfinished?" The old man had apparently not bothered to read the programme notes. "How unfinished can anything be that lasts over an hour?"

"Think carefully," the resource manager said. "You heard only three movements. If that constipated man, with all his spiritual doubts and struggles, had finished the fourth movement before he died you'd have had to sit through another hour . . . What do you say, then? Do you have the patience for the report you've been waiting for? Or are you desperate to go to sleep?"

"I already slept at the concert," the old man joked. "And at my age, there's no need for sleep anyway. If you're still on your feet, come on over. Just give me a few minutes to get organized. Meanwhile, I'd like a yes or no answer: are we guilty or not?"

"Responsible is more like it."

"Responsible for what?"

"I'll tell you later," he said dryly, cutting short the conversation.

It was nearly one o'clock when he arrived at the large luxury apartment. He had been there only once, many years before, during the old man's week of mourning for his elderly wife whom the resource manager had never met and who may not even have been old. The living room had been filled with condolence callers, and the human resources manager, after mumbling a few obligatory words, had retreated to a corner and sat by an illuminated glass cabinet filled with vivid clay and plaster models of the many kinds of bread and baked goods produced by the company during its long history.

Tonight, when he was the only guest, he found himself drawn to the same cabinet. The housekeeper, a small, dark-skinned, white-haired Indian, took his hat, scarf, and gloves and went to call the old man. Did the owner's choice of this woman, the human resources manager wondered, indicate that he considered himself too old for sex?

It took a while for the owner to appear. For the first time since the resource manager had known him, he really did look old. His bath had clearly done nothing to revive him. His tall figure was stooped. The royal pompadour was damp and limp. Dark rings circled his eyes and his face was pale. His feet, clad in old slippers, were dry and veiny. For a moment, the resource manager had the unsettling thought that his boss might be naked beneath his bathrobe. The symphony must have left him feeling drained. Besides wanting to know what his manager had discovered, he seemed anxious to recharge his batteries with the younger man's energy. He filled two glasses with red wine.

"Well?" He raised his glass in a toast. "Is everything clear now? You've identified her? She really did work for us? Tell me what you know."

The resource manager took a sip of the excellent wine and silently handed the owner the thin and by now somewhat dog-eared folder. "Before I tell you anything," he said, "have a look."

The owner reread the newspaper article with an expressionless face; carefully followed the lines of the computer printout with a long, wrinkled finger; and turned to the CV written in the resource manager's hand. Picking up the photograph, he rose, switched on a standing lamp, and went to peer nearsightedly at the cleaning woman, as if seeking to bring her back to life.

The resource manager poured himself some more wine. "Would you say she was an attractive woman?" he softly probed, as he moved to return the folder.

The unexpected question made the owner snatch the folder back for another look. "Attractive? It's hard to say. Perhaps ... but what makes you ask? She has breeding, wouldn't you say?"

Once again the resource manager felt a pang, as if something had been stolen from him forever.

"Breeding?" The word somehow offended him. "What do you mean? What do you see?"

The owner chuckled at the question. "I'm not sure. There's something foreign about her, something ... Asiatic, even though she's fair."

The resource manager had to tell everything. "You wouldn't believe what I've been through," he blurted. "I've been to the morgue on Mount Scopus. In fact, I've just come from there. They wanted me to identify the corpse. I refused. Tell me: Am I responsible for someone I've seen only once in my life? But I found a better solution. Would you like to hear about it?"

The owner sank deeper into his chair and touched the younger man's knee as if to calm him. "Come," he said, moving the bottle of wine out of reach. "It's late. Let's start from the beginning. One thing at a time."

The resource manager was reluctant to forgo the wine. A new thought was forming in his brain. Just look at this old man, he reflected. As wealthy as he is, he insists on being employed by his own company so that he can draw a salary on top of all his profits – none of which will keep him from dying sometime soon. Who knows if he'll be succeeded by a human being like himself or by a faceless board of directors?

He had a feeling of warm intimacy, as if he were in the company of an elderly cousin who, because he had reached the last stage of his life, could be told everything. And so, after praising the wine and wheedling a third glass, he launched into his story, starting with the owner's half-scolding declaration "No choice" and ending with switching off the lights in the dead woman's threadbare shack.

He told it like a detective story, with a beginning, a middle, and an end, knowing that it would be impossible to reveal the whole truth. The night shift supervisor's motives, which had set the plot in motion, would have to remain obscure. Feeling the marvellous wine settle inside him, he was careful to avoid both too much confusing detail and too much oversimplifying generalization. When at last he reached the heart of the matter, he defended the supervisor as though pleading for his own self.

The owner listened patiently, benevolently, letting the resource manager tell the story as he wished. His bathrobe was as ancient as he was. A missing button afforded a glimpse of a dry, waxy body whose thin skin was crisscrossed by blue veins.

The resource manager plunged ahead. He described the corpses he hadn't flinched from looking at, especially the bearded homunculus, and went on to speak of the woman's rumpled bed. With a smile, he apologized for having made it. It was something he'd felt he had to do.

"My compliments," the owner said with an approving glance. "You didn't cut any corners tonight. It's beyond anything I had expected. I must have frightened you this afternoon when I threatened to find someone else if you refused to carry out this task ... "

"That wasn't your only threat," the resource manager said reproachfully. "You also hinted I'd be out of a job."

"Did I?" There was no knowing if the old man's surprise was feigned or if he had merely forgotten. "That article must have upset me greatly."

"I wonder who you had in mind. To replace me with, I mean?"

The old man's eyes twinkled. "There's no shortage of candidates. But why should I replace you when you've demonstrated once again how resourceful you are – especially when you don't want to disappoint me."

The human resources manager agreed with this description. "That's true. It's just as you say. I hate to disappoint. That should help you to understand why I didn't want to let my daughter down tonight. It's enough to have let down her mother."

"She wasn't let down at all," the old man crowed. "She was delighted with the substitutes I found for her. My office manager phoned me before the concert to let me know what a good time she and her husband had."

"She did?" The resource manager felt cheated. "Then you already knew what I've told you ... "

"Some of it. While you were following the progress of my concert, I was following yours. I even phoned the hospital during the interval, but no one could tell me if you'd been there."

"No one could have. But what made you do it?"

"I wanted to see if you were making headway. You still don't realize how upsetting it is to be called inhuman. What is left to us if we lose our humanity?"

"Who else phoned you?"

"The night shift supervisor."

The resource manager was startled. "He did? But when, during the concert?"

"No. Just now, before you came. That's why you had to wait. He couldn't get over his talk with you. He felt the need to confess to me, too. He wasn't sure what you thought of him."

"But why not? Wasn't I fair to him?"

"Too fair. He was much harder on himself than you were on him. But I know him from way back. I'm the last person to be taken in by his sentimentality. He's been with us for over forty years. He was hired by my father when he was a young technical sergeant just out of the army – a good-looking fellow who attracted not only the girls he worked with but older women too. We were constantly bailing him out of trouble. He caused scandals even after he was married and took a long while to settle down. That's why we put him on the night shift: it's quieter there and the workers are tired and have no time for escapades. A few years ago he became a grandfather. He even asked me to be the godfather to one of his grandchildren. And now he falls head-over-heels for some poor Tartar, so much so that he has to fire her to protect himself! While leaving her on the payroll, of course . . ."

The resource manager felt weak from exhaustion. He needed to end this, to return to his mother's, shower, and go to sleep.

"So what line shall we take?" he asked, with the last of his strength. "What should our response be?"

"No line at all." The old man was pale with emotion. "We won't put up any defence. We'll accept the blame, apologize, and offer compensation."

"For what?"

"For the indignity we caused. For firing someone without reason. For our personnel division's ignorance. That's how we'll end all this. Not with some left-handed apology that will just make that son of a bitch dig deeper. We won't offer any version of our own. We'll simply say: 'It's all true. It's our fault. We ask forgiveness and wish to atone.'"

"Atone?"

"Yes. Fully. That's what's called for. I suppose we'll either have to ship her overseas for burial or bring her relatives to a funeral here. We should consider helping her son, too. Her belongings need to be disposed of. Above all, the compensation must be generous."

"But what business is it of ours?" the resource manager protested. "It's the responsibility of the government. We're not to blame for the bombing. Let the government take care of it."

"The government will do what it has to. And we'll stand in for her family and make sure that it does. Of course, the article is nasty. But nasty isn't always wrong. I could cry thinking of that woman fighting for her life without a single one of us even knowing. And then lying unidentified in the morgue, because even our night shift supervisor doesn't notice she's missing! Listen, my friend. I don't want to apologize. I want to do penance. I'm eighty-seven years old and I have no time for polemics. I won't let my or my ancestors' reputation be tarnished."

"You feel that strongly about it?"

"That strongly." The old man raised his voice fiercely, pleased to see the little Indian peer worriedly out from the kitchen.

"But why?" The resource manager no longer knew what he was objecting to. "That woman got an extra pay packet and you treat it as a sin calling for religious expiation."

"Let it be religious expiation. So what? What's wrong with that?"

The resource manager tried to make light of it. "I believe Bruckner's music has left you wallowing in Christian guilt."

"Don't. I slept through most of it."

"That's when our subconscious is most easily affected."

"If it's my subconscious you're worried about," the owner replied, reaching into his robe to scratch his chest, "don't expect it to rely on the government." He was clearly enjoying the conversation. "Yes, I want expiation. I can afford it. And I have just the person for it ... "

"Meaning me?"

"Naturally. Who else? Wasn't it you who asked to change the name of the personnel division to *human resources division*? Your humanity matters to you, too. That's it in a nutshell, my friend. You promised me today to make that woman ... what did you say her name was?"

"Yulia Ragayev," the resource manager whispered, exhausted, suddenly aware of where things were heading.

"Right. So just make Yulia Ragayev your business a while longer until you can give her a proper funeral. You've put hard work and good judgment into this, and there's no reason for you not to continue. We'll show this city that we're not ducking anything and that we deserve forgiveness, even from that journalist. Mark my words: the weasel will faint when he sees how contrite we are. Take the long view, my friend. We have no choice but to see this through. And don't worry about expenses. You'll have all the money you need. I'll be at your disposal day and night, just as I am now ... "

When the human resources manager stepped back out into

the empty street, he felt enveloped by a white blur. In the car, before switching on the ignition and merging with the traffic, he opened a window to let in the cold, and searched for good music on the radio to keep him awake. The only music he could find, however, was too insipid to move him. He put his head down on the steering wheel and waited. The flakes drifting through the window made him realize that the white blur had not come from the wine. A light snow was falling softly on Jerusalem. And just as in his childhood, it gave his spirits a lift.

PART TWO

The Mission

Only in a dream, he thought, could his mother's voice be his secretary's. Then he opened his eyes and realized that it was his secretary, in the apartment, demanding to enter his bedroom, so she could retrieve the cleaning woman's keys. Was her baby still strapped to her? He looked forward to the prospect of planting another kiss on the warm, bald, little head. Knowing, however, that she was at the door and about to turn the knob, he jumped out of bed to defend his privacy. In the past twenty-four hours, his secretary had taken too many liberties. Still, it was late, almost ten. The old man's wine had put the crowning touch on a hard day's work. It was his mother's fault, too. She should never have lowered the blinds or drawn the curtains.

He dressed quickly and asked his mother to shut the living room door. Even a fleeting glimpse of him on his way to the bathroom was more than he wanted his secretary to catch. He didn't intend to exchange a word with her before he had washed and shaved. But he did ask his mother about the snow.

"What snow?"

"Don't tell me it's gone."

She hadn't heard of any snow. There was not a trace of it outside.

When he entered the living room a short while later, washed and shaven yet still embarrassed by the crates and cartons of his possessions that testified to his transient state, he found his secretary, dressed for work and looking official, interrogating his mother.

"What's going on here?" he interrupted.

Naturally, she hadn't come on her own initiative, she told him. She had been sent by the owner, whose unrelenting feelings of guilt made him want to play a more active role in the unfolding saga. The manager was late for work, so he had sent for the keys to the woman's shack, which he wanted to see for himself before deciding on his next move.

"He wants to see that pathetic little room? What on earth for?"

His protests were meant just as much for his mother, who seemed to have become his secretary's accomplice. The secretary, who was delighted to be out of the office, dismissed them with a wave of her hand.

"Why shouldn't he see it? What are you trying to spare him? Let him know how his employees live. As long as he's still alive, a little connection to reality won't hurt him."

He checked an impulse to rebuke her. The fact was that her new critical approach – not only towards him and the night shift supervisor but also, he now saw, towards the owner – made him like her all the more. With a fond look he inquired whether her baby had arrived home safely last night.

"Of course he did."

"I have to tell you, I was genuinely worried he'd be smothered."

"That's one worry I absolve you of."

"You should have brought him with you today, too."

"If you find him that amusing, I can bring him to the office every day. Provided you look after him."

"I'll be glad to. I'd rather chase babies than corpses."

As if her baby had been placed in sudden danger, she stiffened and turned pale. Glancing at her watch, she put down the coffee his mother had served her, sat up in her chair, and dramatically held out her hand for the keys. The resource manager, however, refused to yield them. Ordering her back to the office, he announced that he would personally escort the owner to the shack.

And so that same crisp, clear morning, the old man appeared in the market neighbourhood, dressed in an ermine coat that added to his stature and hale look. His cheeks were ruddy from the cold, the crest of his royal pompadour had sprung back to life; he showed no sign of the previous night's fatigue. Accompanied by his office manager, he followed the solemn resource manager down alleys and lanes until they reached a yard. In broad daylight it had lost all mystery and looked tawdry with its piles of boards and junk. A light film of white assured the resource manager that he hadn't imagined the snow.

He took the keys out of his pocket and unlocked the door like a practised estate agent, guiding the two others inside. A dim, greenish light fell through a heavy, checked curtain that he hadn't noticed before. "Have a look around," he said glumly. "It's just an alcove. I haven't touched a thing, except for some laundry I took down from a line and put in the sink, to keep it from getting mildewed. Actually, I shouldn't have done that either, because only next-of-kin are supposed to handle her belongings. We had better leave it to National Insurance. They are the specialists."

But the old man was in no mood to heed such advice. His large eyeballs glistened with curiosity, as he walked over to a little table covered with the same fabric as the curtains and unceremoniously lifted a bowl resting on it, examining and even sniffing at it. Then he asked the office manager to open the drawers of a chest and rummaged through them with uninhibited thoroughness, inspecting the dead woman's clothing and even getting down on his knees to examine the shoes in the bottom drawer.

"All in all, there's not much here," he said, summing up his impressions. "And what there is looks old and worn. Even so, we'll offer to deliver it to the survivors."

The office manager, who had worked for the owner for many years, nodded doubtfully and stole a look at the resource manager. The resource manager said nothing. He resented this juggernaut of a man turned loose in the same room in which, seated in the straw armchair the night before, he had felt such unusual grief as he repeated the murdered woman's name.

The old owner continued to rummage. After unsuccessfully attempting to decipher the title of a book in Cyrillic characters, he wandered to the kitchenette, studied an electric kettle, turned over a frying pan to contemplate its bottom, sorted out the knives and forks, and moved on to the lingerie that had lain in the sink overnight. Rolling up the sleeves of his fur coat without ceremony, he finished the resource manager's work, wringing out the flimsy panties, nylon stockings, slip, and floral nightgown and carefully spreading them in a bright panoply over the armchair to dry. "We need a good photo-graph of her," he declared.

The office manager gave a start. "Why?"

"For our bakery's memorial exhibition. It shouldn't be only for employees killed in action. Terror victims deserve to be there too."

The resource manager had had enough.

"I'm warning you again," he said, turning sternly to the hyperactive old man. "We mustn't poke around here. And we certainly mustn't take anything. Our company has no personal claims on this woman. We're in enough trouble because that old puppy fell in love. Why look for more?"

The owner was unimpressed.

"Yulia Ragayev." His voice quivered in the greenish light. "What kind of a name is that? Does it sound Jewish to you?"

"Who cares?" The resource manager was getting cross. "All that matters is that she's still on our payroll."

The owner turned to look at the employee, who was nearly fifty years his junior. "What's botherng you?" the old man asked quietly, yet forcefully, putting a hand on the resource manager's shoulder. "What are you getting so worked up about? Have I said what matters and what doesn't? You're right. The important thing is that she's still on our payroll. That's why we'll give her the consideration she deserves. But we can't bury her properly if we don't know where she comes from."

2

At first we didn't notice he was there. When we did, we assumed he must be from the secret service, one of those characters who turn up now and then to scrounge for information, for another intimate detail or two about the dead, not all of whom are always innocent passers-by. We didn't bother to talk to him. He seemed happy enough in his corner, listening carefully to social workers, pathologists, psychologists, assessors, and municipal clerks, all of whom had something to say about the dead, the injured, and their families. Believe it or not, we still have cases ten or more years old whose files we haven't been able to close.

Yet after a while our curiosity got the better of us and we asked him who he was and whom he represented. He apologized for crashing our meeting, which he had only done, he said, to reveal to us the identity of a terror victim. He spelled her name and recited her visa number as if it were his own ID.

At first we didn't realize what this woman had to do with him. Neither her name nor her number meant anything to us. But then someone remembered the unidentified body from the previous week's bombing, which had since been overshadowed by a subsequent one. We had been certain that this body had been transferred to Central Pathology and that we were no longer responsible for it. Now we learned that it was still in Jerusalem. An article that had appeared, or was about to appear, in a local weekly had led this well-meaning man to make the identification. He repeated the name and visa number.

Naturally, we wondered about him. Was he a relative? A friend? A neighbour? Perhaps a lover? Such people sometimes surface post-humously. We've run into all of them before. Yet in this case it was none of the above. To our surprise, the man had not even known the deceased. He was the personnel manager of the Jerusalem bakery in which the victim, an unattached temporary resident, had found work as a cleaning woman. For days no one had noticed she was missing, and the company now wished to make up for the oversight by helping with the funeral arrangements.

The man's request that we allow the bakery to be of assistance, discreetly and without publicity, was more than welcome; it lightened our otherwise gloomy meeting. We immediately directed him to another room with a representative of the Immigration Ministry, who elicited all he knew about the dead woman and took down his phone number and address for further contact. Later we learned that he was divorced and living with his mother – hardly an earthshaking revelation.

The representative of the Immigration Ministry, a woman with flashing eyes and fluent but accented Hebrew, led her visitor to a side room. Since he refused to part with his yellow folder, she had to copy out the deceased's personal details and

CV. When she did not react to the cleaning woman's picture, he took the liberty of asking if she thought the woman was beautiful. "Why shouldn't she have been?" she answered, none too logically, shutting the folder and handing it back to him – a gesture that made him aware of the scent of her perfume. A shiny cell phone appeared in the palm of her hand; into it she relayed his information to her office. "You've done your part," she said to the resource manager. "We'll locate her family and find out how they want us to proceed."

The resource manager gripped her hand lightly. "Just a minute," he said. "My part isn't over yet. I represent a large company that wishes to be involved in this tragic matter and can afford to be. It's in our interest. Our public duty requires us to value every employee, even a temporary cleaning woman. We wish to make it clear that we expect to participate with the government in paying our last respects. You see, we've been attacked in the press and even accused of in-humanity."

"Inhumanity?" She regarded him curiously. The resource manager, who did not want yet another woman to go unremembered, made a mental note of her delicate features while he briefly summarized the article due to appear. Of course, he left out the night shift supervisor's infatuation. It was all just a clerical error.

"Perhaps we're overreacting," he said. "But in times like these, we have to be strict with ourselves and not just with others."

He took down the phone and fax number of her office and, most important, the number of her little cell phone, which quickly vanished into her handbag.

3

The administrative wing was silent when he arrived at his office early that afternoon. His secretary's coat and handbag were not in her room. A note on his desk said: "The baby isn't well. Back tomorrow." She was lying, he thought. Nothing was wrong with the baby. She was taking her revenge for the keys.

He leafed through the papers on his desk. After all the horror stories he had heard that morning at the National Insurance meeting, the usual personnel problems seemed dull and trivial. Not until he stepped into the corridor to ascertain why everything was so quiet did he remember, on hearing muffled voices behind the owner's upholstered door, that a conference had been scheduled to discuss a step-up in production due to a closure imposed on the Palestinian territories – a measure that invariably meant an increase in the consumption of bread, as opposed to more expensive foods. The destruction by the army of several small Palestinian bakeries suspected of harbouring bomb makers had only added to the shortage.

He hesitated before opening the door of the smoke-filled room, where the entire senior staff was gathered around a table set with refreshments – shift supervisors, marketing executives, engineers, transport directors, and several secretaries to record the proceedings. Perhaps, he thought, he could slip inside without arousing attention. But the old man noticed him at once.

"Well, well, at last!" he exclaimed. "We need you. Your secretary has disappeared, and I've made a botch of calculating the cost of extra help."

Although the resource manager signalled that he would prefer to sit in a corner, the owner insisted that he be seated next to him, and immediately asked him about the National Insurance meeting. Once informed of the government's promise to locate the dead woman's family and arrange for her funeral, he relaxed and returned to the subject of bread.

Conscious of the night shift supervisor's anguished gaze, the resource manager took a pen and calculator from his pocket and was soon demonstrating his proficiency at estimating the overhead costs of adding new workers, costs that could be kept down by juggling the bakery's shifts. What more do you want from me, he addressed the supervisor mentally. Didn't I refuse to look at that dead woman's face to avoid the slightest complicity with you? With two sharp pen strokes he crossed out the owner's provisional and totally unrealistic figures.

After the meeting, he returned to his office to work out a more accurate projection. When he phoned his secretary to check on some data, he was told that she was not at home. In a deep, sleepy voice her older son, who seemed to have only the vaguest recollection of having a baby brother, said he didn't know where she was.

The light grew dim outside his window as he worked. The dead cleaning woman was forgotten. So were her lingerie, stockings, flowery nightgown, and thin slip that the owner had set out to dry. So were the National Insurance people and the dozen claylike corpses in the morgue on Mount Scopus. All faded into oblivion as he wrestled with the problem of reorganizing the bakery's three shifts.

Outside, without warning, it began to hail. For a moment he sat there, transfixed by the white pellets striking his desk. Then he slowly rose to shut the window and phoned his ex-wife to make another date with his daughter. She, however, claimed not to know where the child was or when she would return. "What do you want from her now?" she asked impatiently. "Your day with her was yesterday. If you had someone substitute for you, that's your problem, not mine. She and I have plans to spend today and tomorrow together. You can wait for your turn again next week."

"You're being vindictive. We had a terrible accident here. I told you. An employee of ours was killed ... "

She hung up.

He returned to his calculations, but his concentration had gone. His ex-wife's success at packing more and more violence into her sentences was positively frightening. Taking out the phone numbers he had copied down, he dialled the young lady from the Immigration Ministry. Her cell phone identified him at once.

"You'll have to be more patient," she scolded by way of

saying hello. "We've only just managed to trace the name of the woman's former husband, her son's father. We're looking for someone at the embassy to track down his address and arrange to have him informed in person. We've had bad experiences with phone messages getting lost, so please bear with us." She hoped that the authorities would know by the end of the day what to do with the body.

"Of course," he apologized warmly. He dealt with human resources himself and knew these things took time. But that wasn't why he was calling. There was something important he had forgotten to mention. The woman's keys were in his possession. He had been given them by the morgue. If anyone at the Immigration Ministry or National Insurance had need of them, he wanted her to know that he had them.

But the Immigration Ministry did not need the woman's keys. The one urgent matter was deciding where to bury her. Her clothing and personal effects could wait.

"You might try looking for the man who came with her to this country."

"Her Jewish friend, you mean . . ."

"Precisely. You've done your homework. Friend or lover."

"Lover?" She had a refreshing laugh. "What could we do with a lover? We need a next-of-kin who's legally responsible. The only one we know of is her son."

"Isn't he a bit young?"

"Young people can participate in decisions, too, you know."

"You're right. How could I have forgotten him? Yes, that's logical. We'll have to locate him. Just keep me – I mean us – in the picture."

"Don't worry. We can use every bit of assistance. You're in our computer." Graciously, she ended the conversation.

Today's world, the resource manager reflected, could be run perfectly well by secretaries, computers, and cell phones. He was about to return to his figures when he was summoned to the owner's office.

The owner was out, having gone for a medical examin-

93

ation. At his computer sat his office manager, composing the company's response to the weekly. The editor had agreed to display it in a sidebar if it was kept to eighty words.

Looking over her slim, hunched shoulder, the human resources manager read with a sinking heart and eyes blurred with anger.

I wish to thank the distinguished journalist for his shocking and instructive exposé of our company's shameful oversight regarding the death of one of our temporary employees in the recent market bombing. A thorough investigation has revealed the failure to be due to administrative and human errors by our personnel manager. In his name and mine, and that of the entire staff, I wish to apologize and express my deep sorrow. I have given him instructions to cooperate closely with National Insurance in all arrangements and matters of compensation having to do with the dead woman and her family.

He pointed a finger at the screen and counted the words under his breath.

"Ninety-nine," he said. "Since we're limited to eighty, I'll tell you exactly what to do. Delete that unfair, inaccurate, unnecessary sentence that makes me want to scream. Here, this one blaming me for what happened. You'll be left with exactly the right number of words."

He ran his finger across the lines on the screen, this time counting out loud.

The office manager turned to look at him. She had a gentleness that set her off from the brash young secretaries.

"But how can I? If there's an apology with no explanation, we'll be admitting our inability to locate the source of our error."

"In that case," he hissed, "do me a favour and skip the sidebar. You can publish a full response in next week's edition – an accurate and detailed one. I'll dictate to you verbatim the full story of an elderly night shift supervisor's cowardly infatuation with a lonely foreign worker."

"God, no!" She laid a restraining hand on his arm. Her pale, wrinkled face had the remains of an ancient, forgotten beauty. "We couldn't possibly say anything so embarrassing."

"But why accuse me?"

"In the first place, I'm not accusing you. *He* is."

"Then why is *he* picking on me?"

He was doing it, said the office manager, because he wanted the resource manager to be his full partner. Hadn't he promised to make the woman his business? Then let the blame be his business, too. After all, not only was it in his jurisdiction, he was still young – here today and gone tomorrow, if offered a better job elsewhere. Who would remember any of this when he was gone? It wouldn't harm him to take some of the responsibility. The owner, on the other hand, wasn't going anywhere – at least not until the Angel of Death delivered the coup de grâce, as he once put it. His world began and ended in this room, from which he could see the chimneys built by his ancestors. He mustn't be left with the guilt, especially since he was already so tormented by it.

The resource manager listened attentively. Instead of arguing, he felt his outrage yielding. Although he had known the office manager to be an efficient organizer, he had never imagined her to be capable of an original thought. For a moment his mind dwelt on her tall, jaunty husband, whose eyes twinkled with humour. Was it he, with his rugby-ball head, who was behind all this? What, he asked her, changing the subject, were her husband's impressions of his daughter?

"He told you. She has too many gaps in her education."

"That's not what I meant," he said impatiently. "I'm not talking about maths and trigonometry. I'm talking about her."

The old office manager smiled awkwardly. How much time, she parried, had they spent with her?

But the resource manager was insistent. "I liked your husband," he said. "He's a real person."

Her lined face lit up with pleasure. She looked down at the desk, choosing her words carefully.

"I think that he ... like me ... thinks your daughter is a lovely child and far from ... unintelligent. It's just that ..."

"What?"

"She seems to give up too quickly, to surrender without a fight . . . "

"Give up on what?"

"Herself . . . the world . . . perhaps you too. It's self-destructive. My husband says you have to fight for her harder, not to despair of her so easily."

"Despair of her?" The human resources manager was startled. Yet before he could protest, they had slipped past his defences. "I see," he sighed. "I understand . . . in fact, I agree. He's right."

Anxious to get away from this tactful, truthful woman, he dropped his objections to the response to the local weekly.

4

In the Old Renaissance, we heard the jingle of his cell phone. If we hadn't alerted him to it, he would have missed an important call, because he left at once and didn't return. That's how it is with our customers' cell phones. We bartenders are so used to the deafening music the proprietor blasts us with that we no longer hear it, so we do hear the cell phones. Usually this particular customer (he's been a regular these past months) is so tied to his phone that he always puts it down right next to him, bright and shiny, between his beer and his peanuts while waiting for the women to show up. This time, though, he forgot to take it from his overcoat, which we've never seen him wear before. Did he actually think it was going to snow just because it was forecast?

Anyway, he's sitting in his corner with two girls, the one who has a smile for everyone and the good-looking junkie the owner can't get rid of, and an older man, that cultivated fairy who likes to talk to him, when his coat starts making these sounds. It was obvious he didn't hear it and we yelled, "Hey! Don't you know your own cell phone?" He jumped up as if bitten by a snake and answered in the nick of time. "Hang on a second, Miss," we heard him shout, "there's this awful music here." He ran outside, then came back after a while and asked for his bill. We haven't seen him since.

The call had come from the representative of the Ministry of Immigration; she had remembered to keep him in the picture. Despite the late hour, she thought he should know the latest developments. The ex-husband had been informed and was demanding that the woman be buried in her native soil. Although he had neither the time nor desire to arrange for the funeral of someone he no longer cared about, he wanted it done for his son's sake. He personally didn't care if they buried his former wife where she had died. Yet since he had had the good sense to get their son out of "that hellhole," as he scathingly referred to Israel, he felt the boy deserved to have his mother's grave nearby rather than in a distant and permanently dangerous place.

"That's the latest," the efficient immigration ministry representative told him. She had already passed the information on to the National Insurance hotline, along with a request to have the body transferred immediately to Central Pathology, which alone was equipped to prepare it for a long journey. Barring unexpected complications at either end, it should be on its way in forty-eight hours, on a late Friday-night charter flight.

"I see you people know how to get things done." Shivering from the cold, the human resources manager praised her with professional objectivity. Then, pressing the phone to his ear, he retreated to a side street to hear better and to avoid the curious stares of the pub's security guard.

"Yes, we do," the immigration ministry representative replied with a contented sigh, the golden traces of the exotic voice of her childhood accentuated for him the dreams night brings. Alas, she continued, in the past three years her section of the ministry had amassed much experience – although, to tell the truth, it was rare for a body to remain unidentified for so long. It had taken ten days from the time of the bombing to find her next-of-kin. That was far too long. It smacked of chaos and was bad for the country's image. Now they had to make up for lost time, which was why she must know immediately whether the resource manager and his superiors still wished to be involved, even though the government could finish the job without them. There was a budget for such things and a competent staff, and since nobody in the woman's country had heard of the bakery or of any blunder on its part, there was no need for compensation or even an apology. If the resource manager and his company wanted to drop out now, no one would think any the worse of them. If they wished to be part of it, however, National Insurance and her ministry were both in favour of that. It was a lot to have to carry the burden of so much bereavement by themselves. She would appreciate an answer by tomorrow, plus a practical proposal if that answer was yes.

He promised to give her one. "By the way," he added, "you must know that there's a mother, too. She lives in a village somewhere . . ."

"Yes, we do know. We even looked her village up on the map. It's in the middle of nowhere. Contacting her now will just cause further delays – and we have already had too many. We've asked the ex-husband to get in touch with the mother and he said he'd try. Communications are poor there in winter. For the moment, I'd advise leaving her out of it. We can try getting her to the funeral in time."

"Right."

With a plan for the company's proposal now taking shape in his mind, the resource manager allowed himself a glance at the sky, which was bathing him and the street in a radiant light. A full moon had unexpectedly broken free of the winter clouds and seemed to be cruising the heavens as if driven by a brisk breeze. He thought of the cleaning woman and her thin folder that lay in the trunk of his car. At this very minute burly men would be entering the morgue on Mount Scopus, removing her from her refrigerated compartment, wrapping her and tying her to a stretcher, and carrying her in the moonlight to an ambulance, or perhaps a plain pickup truck, for transportation to the Central Pathology Institute near Tel Aviv, her first stop on her long voyage home. He thought of the twelve claylike corpses pledged to science, and of the lab technician's request for an identification.

Which he had refused to give.

Thinking it improper.

Like the night shift supervisor's infatuation.

So that now he would never see the woman at all.

He had an urge to drive to Mount Scopus in the hope of catching a glimpse of her after all. Even were he to get there in time, however, he had forfeited his right. And so, getting into his car, he dialled the owner in order to bring him up to date and let him know of the need for a decision. This time, however, the housekeeper was determined to protect the old man's sleep.

"Do you know who I am?" he asked her.

"I know and I remember you, sir," she answered in her polite Indian English. "But I'm not to disturb the master tonight."

He must be sleeping off his medical examination, thought the resource manager. If he tires so easily, perhaps he'll also tire of this business and let me be – although, he could just as well turn me into a scapegoat . . .

Sounds of shooting came from his mother's apartment. He entered cautiously, sure she had fallen asleep in front of the TV. Yet she was wide awake and smiling, wrapped in a heavy quilt, enjoying an old Hollywood thriller.

"How come you're home so early?" she asked.

"Early?" He glanced with a snort at his watch, went to his room, undressed, put on his flannel pyjamas, went to the kitchen to slice himself a big piece of cake, and returned with the plate to the living room. Perhaps he could still get involved in the movie.

"So how come you're home?"

He told her of the decision to return the woman's body to her homeland so that her son would have a grave to visit.

"That makes sense," his mother said. "That's why you're home early?"

"No. I mean, yes. I'm afraid the old man may ask me to accompany the coffin. He's trying to use me to clear his conscience."

"What do you care? You'll accompany the coffin and see a new part of the world."

"In midwinter? In freezing weather?"

"What of it? This morning you were upset because the snow you thought you saw last night was gone. You'll have all the snow and ice you want there."

He looked at her, half annoyed and half amused.

"Tell me something. Are you trying to get rid of me? Am I a nuisance to you here?"

"A nuisance, no. But it's painful to be reminded."

"Reminded of what?"

"The broken home you've left behind."

5

That night he dreamed he was tossing an atom bomb into his old apartment – a minibomb the size of a ball bearing that could be gripped with his fingers and looked like a toothed, stainless-steel cog. Despite its film of lubricating oil, it was pleasant to hold. With a swift movement he flung it up at the apartment. At first he felt alarmed by what he had done, even if he had no regrets. Yet when he saw that his wife and daughter were unharmed and alive somewhere else, he calmed down. Still, their eyes were red and inflamed, and their resentment made conversation difficult. They'll get over it, he reassured himself, going to inspect the damage. He felt sorriest for the loss of the family albums. A doorman or guard standing in a corridor formed by the debris kept unauthorized persons from ascending to the wrecked upper floors. He was a heavyset, middle-aged man in a double-breasted suit and Mafia-style fedora, and he had set up a small table with a kettle, a plate, and some silverware. With a hand he barred the dreamer's approach.

The human resources manager awoke, turned over on his other side, and dreamed another dream, which he forgot at once.

He was early for work. Going straight to the owner's softly

lit office, he said in a businesslike tone: "Here's the latest. I wanted to tell you last night, but your housekeeper wouldn't let me. As I expected, the woman's husband – her ex, that is – wants her sent back so her son can attend the funeral. He won't let the boy come to Jerusalem; he thinks this country is a hellhole. Her body was transferred to the Central Pathology Institute last night to be prepared for the journey. I don't know how that's done, but I can find out if you're interested. Our consulate there will look after the body once it arrives. They are experts in such things. We simply have to decide where we stand in all this and whether we drop out or continue – and if we continue, how. Both National Insurance and the Ministry of Immigration want an answer this morning."

The old man nodded. His mind seemed already made up. Yet the resource manager went on talking. Now he spoke with emotion.

"Wait. Don't say anything yet. I read your response to the weekly. It was unfair and inaccurate and it made me furious. But then I thought: to hell with it, who cares? Let it stay as it is. I throw that weekly in the garbage without looking at it, so what difference does it make to me what's there? If placing the blame on me – that is, on the human resources division – is any comfort to you, I'll grit my teeth and bear it. I heard you had a major medical examination yesterday. Even though I hope – in fact, I'm sure – that the results will be negative, meaning positive from your point of view, I've decided to spare you the aggravation of another argument."

The old man, having shut his eyes to concentrate on what his favourite young manager was saying, permitted himself a slight smile.

"First of all, thank you. I share your hope, though not your certainty, that the results will be positive – that is, negative, medically speaking. But believe me, even if I were lying on my deathbed, no conversation or argument with you could be aggravating. Behind the executive façade, I see in you a responsible young fellow who can be talked to man-to-man."

The human resources manager shifted in his chair.

"And now," the owner went on, "you'll inform National Insurance and the Ministry of Immigration that our firm will send a representative to accompany our murdered worker to her funeral. In addition, we will make a contribution, or whatever you wish to call it, to her orphan, over and above what he has coming from the government. If the boy's grandmother attends the funeral, she'll get one too. We'll even donate a modest sum – why not? – to the ex-husband, in compensation for his time spent in hell. Believe me, I have the money for it. Too much. I never thought I'd be as wealthy as I've become, especially since the start of all this terror, which makes the whole world want bread and cake. Why not be generous?"

"So as to atone for a cruel and pointless infatuation."

"Cruel? Do you think so?" The old man seemed surprised. "Well, if it was, we'll atone for that too. But who is going to do it? Who'll represent us at the funeral? The answer is obvious. The ideal candidate is sitting across from me. After all, before you separated from your wife and daughter you were happy to be a travelling salesman. What's one more round of travel for you, especially since this time you won't be selling anything? You'll only be giving – and handsomely."

"Excuse me," the human resources manager said sharply. "I didn't separate from my daughter. That was an unkind thing to say."

The owner, aware that his remark had been uncalled-for, looked mortified. Of course! He should never have made it. How could he have been so addlebrained? Rising to his full height, he walked over to the resource manager, seized both his hands, and bent to ask for forgiveness. As if anyone would willingly separate from his child! It was a foolish slip of the tongue, one more sign of advancing senility. Perhaps the resource manager should take a day or two off, not just to prepare for his trip, but to get away from a doddering old man like himself.

He opened his wallet, took out one of its many credit cards, and handed it to the resource manager with a code number. He could spend whatever he saw fit without itemization. Meanwhile he, the owner, would get in touch with National Insurance and with the editor of the weekly – why not? – to let them know about the resource manager's mission. He would also ask his office manager to go through the dead woman's possessions. Anything of material or sentimental value would be packed and shipped with the coffin. The rest would be stored, pending its final disposal, at the bakery. He would simply need the keys to her room.

The resource manager took a key ring from his pocket and removed two keys. "What about those employment figures?" he inquired.

"Never mind them. Your secretary will finish getting them together. As of now, you're temporarily relieved of all your duties in the human resources division. Concentrate on your trip. You're no longer a manager but an emissary. A very special one."

And why not, thought the emissary. *What's wrong with a little vacation?* These past two days he hadn't had a free minute. And even a short trip, especially since he might extend it after the funeral, demanded preparation. His first stop on leaving the bakery was a nearby bookshop, where he bought a guide-book to the cleaning woman's country, complete with a map. Next, he ordered a big breakfast at a café and spread the map out on the table. After finding the provincial capital and the grandmother's village, he phoned the representative of the immigration ministry.

"I don't know if I should be telling you this," he said, "but since you kept me in the picture, I'm returning the favour. Our company is sending me with the coffin, both for sym-bolic and practical reasons, so that I can give the son – and the grandmother too, if she gets there in time – a contribution. You said there's a late Friday night flight. I'll be on it. I was just wondering who's accompanying the coffin at your end. Will it be you or someone else? I wanted to coordinate . . ."

"Who's accompanying the coffin?" The representative of

the immigration ministry sounded nonplussed. "No one is accompanying it. It will fly by itself. Our consul has promised she'll be at the airport."

"The consul is a woman?"

"Yes. An excellent one, too. She was born there and has good connections with the authorities. Believe me, this isn't the first coffin we've sent her."

"Just a minute. I still don't get it. Since when can you put a coffin on an aeroplane as though it were a suitcase? Suppose something happens to it?"

"What could happen? If the plane crashes, the body in the coffin is already dead."

"That's true. But still it seems strange that I'll be its only escort."

"You're not an escort. You're simply on the same flight. Even if you wanted to be one, it's only after you land."

"What about documentation?" His mind was not yet at rest. "There has to be official confirmation of some kind."

"There will be. It's usually given to the head steward or the pilot. But if it will make you feel better, we'll be glad to let you have a copy."

6

By now he was not only disappointed but also worried. What is this, he asked himself. I'm being saddled with a dead woman as if I were her best friend or close relative.

But when he left the café, his mood brightened. The Jerusalem skies had cleared and it was getting warmer. He went to the bank and withdrew a hefty sum in foreign currency, using the owner's credit card. On his way back from the travel agency to his mother's place, he couldn't resist a detour that passed his former apartment building. It was still standing, untouched by his dream. At midday he phoned his ex-wife and said: "Listen to me before you hang up. I know it isn't my day today, but tomorrow night I'm going abroad with the coffin of that cleaning woman. Our company wants me to represent it at the funeral and make a contribution to the orphan. In addition – "

"Get to the point," his ex-wife said.

"I may be away for three days. That means I'll miss next Tuesday again. I'd like to switch to today on a one-time basis."

"We have plans for today."

"Let me have just an hour, or even half an hour. I want to say a proper goodbye before I go. This isn't a holiday or a pleasure trip. It's a long, hard mission on the country's behalf. Who knows that the next explosion in the street won't get you or me?"

"Speak for yourself."

"All right. It may get me."

She yielded and gave him three-quarters of an hour to be with his daughter – provided, of course, that his daughter agreed and had the time for it.

A few hours later, he climbed the steps of the building into which he dreamed he had flung a nuclear weapon, rang the bell, then let himself in with his key. His daughter was sound asleep in her school uniform, her schoolbag tossed on the floor and one red rubber boot still on her foot. Loath to wake her despite his limited time, he looked at her slender figure, which since the divorce had seemed to refuse to mature, with both tenderness and concern. In the kitchen he found a clean plate beside a knife and fork, still waiting for the lunch she hadn't eaten. He took some food from the fridge, put it on the stove to warm, and stood on a chair to reach a small storage space, searching for his old army boots, among other items, which he had put away there, after his discharge.

"What are you looking for, Abba?"

Her face bore the traces of sleep.

"A pair of good boots."

"What for?"

He told her about his mission and the snow and ice that awaited him.

"Wow! I'd love to go with you."

He climbed down from the chair and gave her a big hug. How he'd love to take her! But he couldn't – and even if he could, her mother wouldn't permit it.

He climbed back on the chair and found the boots, which were in good condition. Then he polished them while his daughter dutifully ate her lunch. Now and then he asked her a question about school or took a morsel from her plate. Although she hadn't the vaguest notion of what the gaps in her education were, the solved maths problems and the office manager's English composition had got her good marks.

"Why don't you send me that cute old couple more often?" she asked with an unfamiliar impishness. "They can do my homework all the time."

"They're not so old. Couldn't you see how on-the-ball they were?"

"Sure I could. Maybe that's because they're still in love."

Surprised, he patted her curly head. "You know what? You're pretty on-the-ball yourself."

He could tell from the way her face lit up how seldom he had ever bothered to praise her. Snuggling close to him, she asked about the cleaning woman. He was frank – he described the article due to appear the next day and the supervisor's strange falling in love. Eyes wide with fear, she smiled in spite of herself at his account of his night in the morgue and his refusal to look at the dead woman, even though her beauty was considered special by all who saw her picture.

"Wow!" she repeated excitedly. She wanted to hear more about his trip and to know how much money the woman's son would get.

That, he answered, would have to be decided once he got there. He had no idea what the local currency was worth.

She let out a sigh. How she would have liked to go with him! Not just because of all the snow, but also to see the woman's son. Was he good-looking like his mother? To think he had lived right here in Jerusalem . . .

They talked on and on. Groping his way, he sought to assure her that he would never give up on her and that she should never despair of him. The afternoon sun outside the window was sharpening its palette of colours as the day grew brighter. His daughter's simple but honest questions and his candid replies had forged a new closeness between them. When his ex-wife came home early, he didn't grumble or complain. Hanging his boots over one shoulder, he simply said, "All right, I'm off. You didn't give me as long as you said you would, but that just made every minute worth more."

He phoned his secretary from his car to ask what was new in the office and whether anyone had phoned for him. As usual, however, she had taken advantage of his absence to escape to her baby. The office manager wasn't in, either. Dialling the switchboard operator, he was told she had no idea where they were. It was as if the entire staff had taken the day off along with him. In the end, he reached the office manager on her cell phone and let her know how seriously he had taken her advice and how his daughter had responded.

There was a new tone of respect in her voice. "I'm so glad you called," she said. "Imagine where we are now. In her room!"

"Yulia Ragayev's?"

"Yes. My husband is helping me sort her clothes and belongings. Where are you? If you're in the neighbourhood and have a few minutes, come see what we've set aside for you to take and what goes into storage. We don't want you to complain that we've saddled you with too much."

This is turning into a collective mania, the resource manager thought with a grin, setting his car on a course for the market. The old man has flipped out and is taking everyone with him. Even the ever-brighter sun, dipping westwards as it tinted the Knesset building in the Valley of the Cross with a coppery wash, seemed to be celebrating his mission. By now he was familiar with the dead woman's neighbourhood and drove confidently into its maze of teeming streets.

It was his third visit in the past forty-eight hours. The checked curtain had been taken down from the open window, which now flooded the shack with the glow of the winter afternoon and the smells of the neighbours' cooking. The room had been turned upside-down. Bread cartons from the bakery lay on the floor, filled with the items chosen for storage. A handsome leather suitcase on the table held those reserved for the resource manager.

"I hope you haven't given me her underwear and night-dress too," he said with a crooked smile. "Let's not go overboard."

The office manager let him inspect the suitcase as though he worked for airport security. Thorough as always, she ex-plained each item. Folded at the bottom was a long white dress, perhaps the woman's wedding gown. Next came five embroidered blouses and a pair of expensive leather boots. The checked curtain had been deemed worthy of repatriation too, because of its high-quality fabric. It had been used to wrap the Cyrillic book and the wall sketch. On top of the pile lay a packet of papers, and next to them the dead woman's reading glasses and a small copper bell that chimed pleasantly when rung.

"Tell me," the resource manager inquired. "Have you by any chance found a good snapshot of her for our memorial corner?"

They hadn't. There was only a small album with several old photographs, which he decided to take in his hand luggage. Mounted on heavy paper and looking like old postcards, these were snapshots of a young woman: in some, she stood on a porch, looking out at a distant field; in others, she sat in a room, holding a half-naked baby. She did not resemble the computer image etched in his memory.

"These photos look old," he said. "Her ex-husband can tell us if they're of her. She might be the baby and this could be her mother. The tilt of the eyes is more pronounced in the baby ..."

He blushed, and added with a slight stammer, "After all, I ... I don't suppose it matters. It's all absurd anyway. In two days' time, we'll bury her and be done with it."

The husband's look of compassion turned to one of

concern, as if there might be gaps in the resource manager too. What measures, he asked practically, had been taken to ensure efficient communication when he was abroad? He advised taking a satellite phone. "If the old man has given you a blank cheque," he said, "don't scrimp. A satellite phone costs more to use, but you can count on getting through. Anyone travelling to a strange and unreliable country in mid-winter, especially with a corpse in a coffin, ought to be in touch with more than just the netherworld."

When we saw that God had made a miracle and brought back the man, who was now carrying a suitcase, we all shouted, "Abba, Abba, come quick! The man's in the yard, go and see what he wants." Father put a bookmark in his Talmud and ran to ask when he could visit Yulia at the hospital. But the man was annoyed and said, "What kind of a neighbour are you not to know that she was killed in the market bombing ten days ago?" He had told us she was only injured, he said, because he didn't want to frighten us.

Every one of us six sisters (we're all for one and one for all!) saw our father turn pale and start to tremble. He took the death of our lonely neighbour very hard, as if she had been his best friend. Oy vey, we thought – none of us said it out loud – it's worse than we imagined. If our father is so sad, he must have been in love with that foreign woman. And though now we pray to God to avenge her blood, the sooner the better, it's a good thing for mother, who is always so sad, that our nice, beautiful neighbour is dead.

7

On Friday morning he awoke earlier than usual and full of foreboding. Although he'd been determined to throw out the weekly without looking at it, his anger and curiosity got the better of him.

Not a word in the article had been changed. It was the same nasty piece he had read originally. Beneath a blurry photo-graph of him, like a knife in his heart, was the caption: *He owes his job to his divorce. You goddamn weasel,* he whispered. *You and your goddamn editor.*

The owner's response, in a black-bordered sidebar, was the same ninety-nine words he had seen over the office manager's shoulder. Do not suppose, my dear and obedient lady, the resource manager thought, that all your English compositions and solved maths problems will keep me from making you pay for this . . .

He was about to throw the paper away when he noticed that there was indeed something new, a note from the editor expressing satisfaction with the owner of the company's admission of guilt and promise to make amends. The editor wished to praise his very accomplished and courageous old friend by publicly disclosing that he had for years been supplying the weekly with newsprint at a favourable price. Although it was common to accuse the paper of sensational-ism, what better proof could there be of the pure profession-alism of its motives? What better defence of his own integrity than his willingness to criticize a company he depended on? The weekly would follow up on the bakery's apology and generous pledge in its next issue.

This encomium for the old owner only heightened the resource manager's resentment. The next issue? No, thank you. Count him out. He wasn't giving any follow-ups. They could print their filth without him.

He crumpled the article, along with the rest of the news-paper, into a big ball and tossed it into the large wastepaper basket he had bought for the apartment on moving into it. "Don't worry," he told his startled mother. "It's not your regular paper. It's the weekly with that idiotic piece I showed you on Tuesday. I didn't think you'd want to read it again."

A seasoned traveller like him didn't need to prepare exten-sively for this trip, so he had time to drop by the office. As the administration wing was mostly deserted on Fridays, he found no one there to tell about his mission. The old man's office was empty, too, except for a young typist taking down voice mail messages.

Before returning to the parking lot, he decided to see what was new in the bakery. Perhaps the night shift supervisor had been moved to the day shift to chill his ardour. Without having to be told, he asked for and put on his white cap and smock. Yet except for one, all the ovens were cold and empty and the production lines mostly silent. But the cleaning staff were out in force. Friday was the day when, besides tidying up as usual, they also scrubbed the machinery, in preparation for the full resumption of work on Saturday night. If that old puppy hadn't fallen in love, the resource manager thought, there would be one more cleaning person here now, an earnest, lonely woman in her prime, with stunning Tartar eyes. No one on the work floor now lived up to her image.

Before leaving he took two warm loaves of hallah from a crate, remembering the special taste of the bread the night shift supervisor had given him. He would charge those to the owner too.

He returned home, ate lunch, put on his track suit, turned out the lights in his room, and lay down for a nap, even though he would be forgoing his weekend bar-hopping tonight. He had a 4 a.m. flight to catch to a cold, foreign land, and though he had a gift for dozing on aeroplanes, a few extra hours' sleep wouldn't hurt.

Indeed, he slept soundly, without disturbing dreams. The presence of his mother, asleep in the next room, made his slumbers even calmer. Rising, he packed his old carry-on bag, a small suitcase that could be taken as hand luggage, like an extension of himself, though it also had a secret compartment for extra capacity. He considered packing his overcoat in the suitcase with the woman's belongings; but decided against blurring the line between the living and the dead (besides, if he forgot his coat and left it in there, it would become part of her estate). Then he drank a cup of English tea with his mother, eating a slice of the bakery's bread instead of his usual cake; and went off to a downtown café for his weekly meeting with two married friends of his. This meeting was their way of reliving their bachelor days before taking up the family obligations of the Sabbath.

The winter was back. An overcast sky sprayed thin rain. He

returned to his mother's and put on his army boots, thinking, *I'll consider this one more stint of reserve duty*, then went to see the owner of the company. It was eight o'clock and the house was full of guests: grey-haired sons and daughters, fat grand-children, and tall, stringy great-grandchildren. News of his mission must have preceded him, for he was received with warmth when introduced to a representative selection of the owner's offspring. Then the two of them closeted themselves in a small library with a desk and couch, over which copies of the weekly were shamelessly scattered. The praise lavished by the editor on his newsprint supplier had banished all the accusations of inhumanity from the owner's mind.

In response to his request, the resource manager was given a handsome leather case with a satellite phone – or did it work by starlight? – that came with a charger and a list of useful phone numbers, including that of Central Pathology, in case he was asked difficult questions. "Never fear and feel free to use it," the old man commanded him, though every call would set him back five dollars per minute, not including the VAT. "Don't economize for my sake. I'll want to be part of every decision. My bank manager has informed me that you've already withdrawn a handsome sum. I like that. It's the right approach. Always tell yourself: 'The owner of the company is loaded. His family won't starve when he dies.'"

He laid a cautious hand on the younger man's overcoat, as if to see if it offered sufficient protection against the cold. Satisfied with its quality, he turned his attention to the question of a hat. Would his emissary like an old fur one. It looked cumbersome, but it might come in handy in a snow-storm.

The resource manager declined. "Then at least," said the owner, "leave your car in my garage. I'll have my chauffeur drive you to the airport and help you with the extra packages."

"What extra packages? All her things are in the suitcase."

"Hers, but not ours. We're sending her family a symbolic gift: a carton of stationery, notebooks, and binders, and another of cakes, rolls, and our finest breadcrumbs and croutons. Let her friends and family, and especially her son, know where she worked and what she produced."

"But she didn't produce anything. She was a cleaning woman."

"And isn't our cleaning staff part of the production line?" the old man scolded. "You're the last person I'd expect to hear that from."

"Look, this is getting to be silly. I'm not lugging cakes and breads thousands of miles."

"You won't have to lug anything. You're simply in charge of the shipment. The consul will be expecting you and will see to everything. I've spoken to her and she'll happy to be of service."

The resource manager threw up his hands. There could no longer be any doubt. Atonement was turning into lunacy.

"A well-intentioned lunacy, though," the owner said. He smiled, steered the resource manager back to the noisy living room, and signalled to the chauffeur that it was time to set out for the airport. The chauffeur seemed so at ease with the owner's family that the resource manager wondered if he might be a distant cousin or illegitimate grandson. The astonishing thought occurred to him that perhaps the old man was intending to adopt him too.

8

At the check-in counter he was handed, along with his boarding card, an envelope from the Ministry of Immigration. A note attached to it, addressed "To the Personnel Manager," said, "As per your request to be kept in the picture."

Touched, he went to sit in a far corner of the departure hall. I'm about to find out things about that woman that she never knew herself, he thought, opening the envelope and extracting with a momentary qualm a photocopy of the Central Pathology Institute's medical report. Written in the Cyrillic alphabet, its crowded lines suggested that it was more than just a death certificate. Most likely, it contained a description of her embalming.

The white pop of a flashbulb interrupted him. A passenger standing with his back to him had just taken a picture of the departure gate.

The charter flight was operated by a foreign airline. It was half full and offered only one class of service. Seated in the front, he surveyed the passengers filing by him, hoping to spot one who looked capable of both reading the medical report and keeping it confidential. Judging by their bags and packages, most of those boarding the aeroplane were either guest workers going home on holiday or new immigrants revisiting their native land. Even if he found someone to read the report, what were the chances that person could explain it to him in comprehensible Hebrew? And so he changed his mind and sat back in his seat, just as the passenger with the camera – now slung around his neck – passed him with a companion, a vaguely familiar-looking man who flashed him a smile.

And what did it really matter? What in the report might he need to know? The only detail of consequence was how long the body could remain unburied, which was in any case a problem for the consul, not for him. After takeoff he folded the document, stuck it in his pocket, released his safety belt, ate some of the tasteless meal, and switched off his reading light. He was unable, however, to relax. Suppose the consul wasn't at the airport to greet him – what would he do then? Although the medical report endowed him with a measure of authority, he wasn't sure it would be wise to display it.

He thought about the dead passenger in the baggage hold, which might be directly beneath him. Once again he whispered her name, as he had done that night in her shack. *Yulia Ragayev*, he murmured sternly, though not without pity. *Yulia Ragayev, what more must I do for you?*

He rose and went to the toilet, glancing at the other passengers as he passed down the aisle. Most were asleep beneath their blankets. Even those with earphones seemed to be listening to the music in their dreams. As he groped his way in the darkness, a man rose from his seat and threw an arm around him, blocking his progress.

"You called me a weasel?" It was the photographer's companion. "Well, then, here I am, the whole beast from head to tail. I'm delighted to make your acquaintance. This is my photographer. In the end we've met in the skies – and in a completely new spirit. We've come to cover your mission of atonement for our paper. Don't worry, this time we're on your side. We definitely won't bite."

A sleeping passenger opened his eyes and groaned. The resource manager stared down and said nothing. He wasn't surprised. In fact, he had suspected as much. Shaking off the journalist's embrace, he said in a steely voice:

"The honest reporter, eh? We'll see if you're capable of it. I'm warning you, though – you and your photographer had better steer clear of me."

Before the journalist could reply, he found himself pushed lightly backwards. Continuing to the toilet, the resource manager locked the door and stared hard at the mirror. Had it been possible to use the satellite phone, he would have called Jerusalem to protest at the two stowaways. And yet he couldn't deny that their presence also pleased him. The old man must have offered to pay their way. Anything to assure that his restored humanity be on the record, if only in a Jerusalem weekly that few read and even fewer thought about.

The resource manager put his shaving kit on the sink, lathered his face, and ran a razor over it. A predawn shave to make himself look presentable to his troops had always been his habit in the army.

Uh-oh! Here comes another coffin. Quick, go and get an officer to decide what to do with it before it's too late again! Should we send it back to the plane until there's someone to receive it or should we do it the honour of taking it to the terminal? Could someone please tell us what's happening over there in the Holy Land? Who are all these dead they keep sending us? Is it some kind of money-making business?

Now the passengers are disembarking. In shock from the cold, they run for the little bus. Did that coffin come with family or friends, or with some government official, so that we don't have a repeat of the last time, when one arrived by itself and sat for two months with no one to claim it? In the end we had to bury it ourselves, next to the runway.

Still, even if none of us wants to admit it, it's just as well that something happens now and then to break the boredom. A town like ours can get pretty depressing; our little airport never sees the fine ladies and gentlemen who fly around the world in the movies. We're in the sticks out here. There are five flights a day and each takes off again right after landing. The passengers disappear quickly. At our airport there are no shops, no businesses. Even the little café that opens for each flight shuts down again at once. The only exercise the waitresses get is in the officers' beds. And how long can anyone drag out the pointless inspections of the new arrivals and their luggage? A coffin, you have to admit, is more interesting and comes with some action. Provided, of course, that it's disposable.

But here comes the officer, jumped out of bed with a new medal on his chest, bought last week in the market. He's telling the policeman on duty to move over so that he can check the passports himself and sniff out any rat. It takes someone with experience to pick out at a glance the culprit who's trying to slip away.

9

Well, what of it, thought the emissary when he was taken out of line and asked – most politely, to be sure – to report to the baggage terminal. The consul will soon come to relieve me of this responsibility that I should never have taken upon myself. And if she's late, I have my satellite phone. Besides, I'm not alone. The journalist and his photographer don't have a story without me.

He was not and never had been a coward, neither in the army nor in his travels as a salesman, and so it was with confidence that he descended to the baggage terminal in the basement of the airport – a converted military base – and strode down its narrow corridors. With an expression of amusement he followed an officer into a grim-looking cubicle that might have been a room for transit, interrogation, or even detention. Putting down his carry-on bag, he took the liberty of sinking into a chair, as if he had just covered the distance from the Holy Land on foot, meanwhile hastening to wave his three baggage stubs as a way of requesting the rest of his luggage. Only when the leather suitcase and two cartons arrived and he identified them with a nod did he consent to show the document in his possession. Whatever was in it, he assumed it would be enough to begin the negotiations that the consul would conclude.

Absorbed in reading, the officer absentmindedly fingered his new medal. A red ribbon, tied to his cap by his latest lover, dangled before his eyes. It was impossible to tell whether he found the document intriguing or simply too difficult to follow. Just then, though, the deep silence in the cubicle, which was definitely beginning to seem like a detention room, was broken by footsteps and the sound of something heavy being dragged. Cries of warning mingled with stifled laughter. The door burst open and the coffin entered slowly, gripped by four policemen under the direction of an old porter.

The resource manager shut his eyes and breathed deeply. *Just keep calm*, he told himself. *Think of the funny story this will make one day. The bars have now closed in Jerusalem. If that woman I was hoping to meet came looking for me, she's found someone else by now. But that's all right, too. I'm on a short, simple mission and I only need to wait patiently for the consul. She'll come, no doubt about that. I've mentioned her twice to this officer, who has almost finished reading the letter. Even if her name meant nothing to him, her title speaks for itself. "Consul" is an international word and an old one. There were consuls in Roman times.*

The officer rose and folded the document. He briefly debated what to do with it, then returned it with a slight bow, said something in his own language, and signalled to the resource manager that he would return shortly, then departed, after unexpectedly locking the door behind him.

The human resources manager rose and took out his satellite phone, which he had shielded until now from possibly covetous eyes. Trying not to look at the coffin, which seemed to loom larger and larger, he dialled the consul. The line was crystal-clear and the call was answered by the consul's husband, who, it turned out, also served as her aide-de-camp. His calm baritone inspired trust: it was the voice of an old, experienced hand. "Ah, it's you! At last! We've been waiting for a sign of life from you. It's a good thing those two journalists told us you were on the plane. Otherwise, we'd have thought that you'd missed the flight and the coffin had come without you. Don't worry, though. We're here in the airport. Everything is under control. My wife inquired why you had been separated from the other passengers. It's actually quite simple. There's nothing mysterious or personal there. A few months ago there was a problem with a coffin from Israel that no one came forward to claim. In the end, they had to bury it themselves. That's why, when you made the mistake of saying you were this coffin's chaperone, they were determined to keep you close by."

"I didn't say anything. They already knew – don't ask me how. But it doesn't matter. Just get us out of here."

"Us?"

"Me and the coffin."

"Of course. In a jiffy. We're just waiting for a signed commitment from the family as to the time and place of the funeral. The coffin can't be released without it."

"But her husband ... I mean her ex ..." The flustered emissary had begun to stammer. "Isn't he with you?"

"Of course. He's right here. He's prepared to go to the cemetery and do the honours right now. But he's not the problem. It's his son, who is refusing to cooperate. The boy insists that we wait for his grandmother. He doesn't want his mother buried without her."

"But where is she? Why didn't you bring her too?"

"That's the whole point. She lives far away and doesn't know that her daughter is dead. She went on a pilgrimage to a monastery several days ago and can't be informed until she gets back."

"But that will take time. How do you know when, or even whether, she can get here? Who gave the boy the right to decide?"

"He's the next-of-kin. He's authorized to sign for the coffin and its burial."

"How can he be authorized at his age?"

"He is. Apart from the grandmother, he's the only blood relation."

"But how old is he?"

"Thirteen or fourteen, though he looks older. He's not a child any more. And unfortunately, he's a complicated type. There's a delinquent side to him. It's hard to know what's going on inside him that's making him so stubborn. He may be trying to extort additional benefits from our government. In any case, we can't do anything without him."

"But what about me?"

"Where are you?"

"I don't know. Somewhere in the baggage terminal. In a room with the coffin."

"With the coffin? Those dumb police have gone too far. I'm terribly sorry ... why didn't you tell me before? The consul will have you released at once, or at least transferred elsewhere."

"It's no big deal. Just try to do it quickly."

"Of course. The bastards have taken you hostage to cover their asses. But don't worry, we'll get you out of there. If they need a hostage, I'll take your place."

"I'm not worried. I'm fine and in no hurry. Just don't forget me."

"Of course we won't. This is an excellent phone connection. Your voice sounds as if it were inside my head."

"That's because I'm using a satellite phone that doesn't depend on the mercies of the local system. It's plugged right into the sky."

"Well, then, you have no cause for concern. Just give me

your number."

The conversation having ended, the resource manager went over to the coffin. He had now devoted three whole days to this woman, labouring faithfully on her behalf after giving his impulsive word to make her anonymous death his business. So far he had kept it. Now, in a locked room, the two of them had finally met. Although it wasn't the face-to-face encounter proposed to him in the morgue, it seemed intimate enough. It's a pleasure to meet you, he smiled. I'm the manager of the bakery's personnel department, better known as its human resources division – and you, Yulia Ragayev, having worked as a cleaning woman there, have all the rights of a terror victim as defined by National Insurance.

He placed a firm hand on the coffin to see what it was made of and to test the strength of its joints. A sleeping angel, the lab technician had called her. Was that just to goad him into identifying her, or had that expert on corpses truly detected in this one a rare, soul-stirring beauty? Now, it lay a few feet from its captive chaperone, itself a captive in the strangest of limbos, trapped between worlds, detained in a baggage terminal that was no longer in his country and not yet in hers. If he could open the coffin, he would gladly take a farewell look. Perhaps a close-up view would tell him if the Tartar eyes were real or imagined. The state of her body would not deter him. He was young and could take it. He had the pluck and imagination to reconstruct her beauty even if it was gone.

But suppose that the coffin, which had been pushed against the wall, was locked on its far side? And the room's single window tall and set high in the wall, did not look as if it could be opened. What if there was a bad smell? He decided that it would be best to take his leave of her with words alone, in a musing, questioning eulogy. What did you want from us, Yulia? What did you hope to find in the hard, sad city that killed you? What kept you there when you could have gone home with your only son?

Had the lid of the coffin lifted and the woman inside it sat up to reply, he would not have been fazed. After all, he had everything she might need. Her good clothes were in the suitcase for her; there was also cake and bread if she was hungry, and even notebooks, pens, and pencils she could use to jot down her impressions of dying while they were still fresh . . .

The satellite phone rang, interrupting his thoughts. It was the consul's husband again, still worried about him. "If you're feeling anxious, relax. We haven't forgotten you. If we can't get the little pain-in-the-ass to sign, we'll find someone to relieve you by the coffin."

"I'm not anxious and don't you be, either," the resource manager replied. "I never thought this mission would be simple. Take all the time you need. I'm fine for now."

He looked for the light switch. Unable to find it, he put the two cartons on top of the suitcase, propped his feet on them, covered his eyes with the black eye mask he had been issued on the aeroplane, and lay back to get some rest.

10

The eye mask did its job, which was fortunate, because it took the consul's husband a while to get him released. The suspicious officer, fearful of being saddled with another coffin, was loath to exchange his foreign hostage for a local one.

The resource manager was dozing when he felt a friendly hand on his shoulder. It belonged to the consul's husband, a sturdy man of about seventy with a head of grey curls, who had come to keep his promise. An ex-farmer with hearty looks and a bluff manner, he seemed to have come straight from the fields. Pulling off his boots and shaking the snow and mud from them, he removed several layers of clothing, spread them casually on the coffin, took a pair of reading glasses from his pocket, whipped out the weekend edition of a Hebrew paper that had arrived on the flight from Tel Aviv, and declared his readiness to settle in for the duration. Only then did the officer, persuaded the substitution was genuine, permit

121

the emissary to exchange the gloomy terminal for a foggy morning.

Climbing back up to the ground floor, he found himself locked in a second time, the small airport having been shut down between flights. A key had to be sent for before he could exit and join the group waiting for him beneath a small canopy. A flashbulb popped as he cautiously made his way between banks of black slush. He looked up to see the grinning photographer. He was not, he thought ruefully, going to have much privacy on this trip.

The tall consul, dressed in a black fur coat, a red woollen cap, and galoshes, made him think of a fairy godmother – or of an old peasant, like her husband, magically transported from some penurious henhouse or barn to a position of state. Underneath the canopy, which stood in an icy expanse devoid of a single building or tree – or anything at all except an old, one-winged military aeroplane – she embraced him warmly, apologized for the treatment he had received, declared that the authorities' apprehensions were nevertheless not unfounded, and introduced him to the deceased's husband, Mr Ragayev, a tall, gaunt engineer with dull eyes in a haggard face. His obsequious bow suggested that he had been informed by the consul or her husband, or perhaps even by the weasel, of the compensation sent by the bakery from the land of horrors he had left behind. And yet even though he had since remarried he seemed in no mood to forget the grief and insult meted out to him by the woman who had abandoned him and was now returning in a metal box. Since she was deaf to his complaints, he was forced to voice them to her chaperone.

"Tell him to be quick," the resource manager whispered to the consul, who was translating. A brightening dawn flung glittering swords at a low, leaden sky. He was only now beginning to grasp what the arctic cold of this country was like. Moreover, the consul was finding it difficult to be concise, since she felt compelled to defend the country she represented against the ex-husband's bitter reproach that that country had irresponsibly extended the visa of a woman to whom it would offer only poverty, solitude, and death. Once that peculiar friend of hers had fled back home in disappointment, the gaunt engineer complained, his ex-wife should never have been allowed to remain only to perish in a blood feud that was none of her concern. And the most absurd part of it (the consul was translating as fast as she could) was that he was now expected to take charge of the body of the woman who had two-timed him! He realized, of course, that the consul's government was paying the costs. But this was the least it could do after causing the needless death of a foreign worker whom it had neglected to expel ... and who would pay for all his time and mental anguish? He was a busy engineer and not in the best of health; truth be told, it wasn't sorrow or compassion that he felt for his ex-wife, but anger and humiliation. Of course, he was a grown man and could cope. But what about his son? The boy was so devastated by the death of the mother who had sent him back to his native land that he had refused to bury her without the presence of his grandmother, thus forcing him, the father – as if he hadn't got enough on his mind! – to twist the boy's arm for the sake of a woman who had let him down ...

His grievances listed, the gaunt man seemed content. The shadow of a smile flitted over his pale face as he lit a cigarette, inhaled deeply, and blew out perfect smoke rings. A moment later, however, the cigarette had flown from his mouth and lay glowing on the ice. Shutting his eyes, he turned red and doubled over in pain, racked by a fit of coughing that caused him to leave the cover of the canopy, tear open his jacket, vest, and shirt, and bare his gasping chest to the elements.

"Don't let him fool you," came a whisper as the paroxysm continued. It was the weasel – who, in all the excitement, had forgotten the resource manager's warning to steer clear. "It's just an act to make you up the ante."

"But where is the boy?" the emissary wondered. He was the only person there without a hat and his bare, closely cropped head was pounding from the cold.

The journalist took him by the arm, turned him around,

and steered him towards a parking lot on the far side of the canopy. He now saw that the small airport was near a city: a skyline of buildings, spires, and domes gleamed through the fog. Cheered by these signs of civilization, perhaps even of culture, he followed the journalist to a van where a driver was dozing at the wheel. In the back seat, he glimpsed through a grimy window a young passenger in overalls, sitting with his head tossed back not in sleep but in a rigid gesture of defiance.

At long last, thought the resource manager. Her own flesh and blood!

The journalist's heavy, padded boots, part of an outfit he had purchased against the polar weather, crunched the ice. Approaching the van, he rapped lightly on its window to let the boy know someone wished to meet him.

But the boy seemed in no mood to meet anyone or even to leave the car – and when scolded for his indifference by the man at the wheel, he merely looked away and jammed down the earflaps of the old pilot's cap he was wearing. At this, the driver stepped outside, opened the back door, yanked his young passenger from the car, and disdainfully knocked off his cap. In silent fury, his eyes filled with tears, the boy threw himself at his assailant and pulled his hair.

The emissary's heart went out to the youngster. So this was the young man mentioned in the job interview he had conducted. In the midst of the fracas he made out a winsome Tartar tilt to those light-coloured eyes, the harmonious product of a rare racial mixture. My secretary is right, he scolded himself. I live inside myself like a snail, beauty and goodness passing me by like shadows.

"What was that?" the weasel asked, sensing his agitation. "Did you say something?"

"No, nothing." He shrank from the probing antennae that, instead of keeping their distance, were latching onto him more and more.

His coughing fit concluded, the boy's father hurried over to break up the fight. Yet the boy, too enraged to acknowledge defeat, now threw himself in despair at his father. The tall consul, confident of her powers, went over to lend a hand. The father did not need assistance, though. Dragging his son to the edge of the parking lot, he subdued him single-handed. The photographer, convinced, so it seemed, that nothing was real unless filmed, popped flashbulbs at them as they wrestled.

"They don't get along," the consul explained to the emissary. "When we came to tell the boy about his mother, he wasn't home. Neither his father nor his stepmother knew where he was or when to expect him. Since returning from Jerusalem a few months ago, he's been depressed. He hangs out in the streets, plays truant from school, and appears to have fallen in with criminal elements. His father didn't want to break the news to him. Besides fearing a hysterical reaction, he didn't think he would be believed. He wanted us to do it, and we had to wait until midnight for the boy to come home. At first, as the father predicted, he was in a state of denial. He had just received a letter from his mother; how could she be dead? He even took it from his pocket to show us. It had been written a day or two before the bombing and said she was postponing a planned visit from winter to spring because she had to look for a new job. We tried to reason with him. We showed him the postmark and swore to him she hadn't suffered. But the more we talked, the more he clammed up; we could see that he wanted us to go away. It was only when my husband told him that the coffin was arriving in two days and that he would have to sign for it and authorize the funeral that he changed his tune. He started to cry and scream at us, to curse his own mother, and to threaten that he wouldn't sign anything. We could bury her in the market where she died! We could burn her body and scatter the ashes in Israel! He wasn't going to solve our problems for us. And if she did have to be buried here, his grandmother could sign the papers. She had sent his mother to Jerusalem – now let her answer for her blood."

"*She* sent her to Jerusalem? How's that?" asked the resource manager.

"Who knows? You can't tell what he's thinking. Not even his father can explain him to us. We're stuck with him ..."

"Wait a minute." The resource manager's eyes were still on the wrestling match, which was now coming to an end. "How old did you say he was?"

"Fourteen at most. But he's mature for his age, mentally and physically. You'll see for yourself. Being so isolated in Jerusalem gave him a tough skin. I'm told his mother worked the night shift."

"That wasn't our doing. She asked for it because it paid more."

"Whatever. I understand. But he spent those nights roaming the streets and falling in with a bad crowd."

"A good-looking boy like that attracts people," remarked the journalist, who seemed to consider himself an equal partner in the conversation. "Just look at my photographer: he can't stop shooting him. I tell you, he'll be the lead picture in my article."

"Wonderful!" The consul, unaware that the newspaper was only a local weekly, was impressed.

The resource manager turned and strode towards the boy, who was now gripped tightly by his father. In the icy, intensifying light, his pure, finely chiselled face and wet, wonderfully bright eyes were more pronounced. The arch in their upper corner, like a prolongation of the brows, made the emissary's heart skip a beat.

"I still don't get it," he remarked to the consul, who had followed him. "Couldn't you have found the grandmother and brought her here?"

"What are you talking about?" The consul was flabbergasted. "This is a big, backward country and communications are rudimentary. It was all we could do to get word to her via someone from a nearby village. She's gone on a pilgrimage for her New Year and won't return for several days."

"Well, then," the resource manager said briskly, "we'll wait until she does and then fly her here."

"How will you do that?" The consul's astonishment was

growing. "Do you have any idea where you are? There's no airport anywhere near her."

"How about a helicopter?"

"A helicopter?" The consul let out a groan. "I can see you're in dreamland. What helicopter? Just think of the distance. Who'll pay for it?"

"We'll do our share," the emissary said cautiously. He had an urge to meet the dead woman's old mother. "A few months ago, I read about a helicopter being dispatched to an oil rig in the open sea, to bring the father of a soldier killed in action to his funeral."

The consul was growing exasperated. "There's no comparison! She wasn't a soldier killed in action. She was a temporary resident of doubtful legal status. I'm warning you for the last time: Don't expect the world you're in now to resemble the one you've come from. Conditions are different here. They're tough, and in winter they're downright primitive. Things you think should be possible aren't. Forget it!"

"What do you mean, forget it?" The resource manager was losing patience, too. "We're talking about the legitimate request of a boy who's lost his mother. Being a temporary resident didn't keep her from dying in Jerusalem. Like it or not, we're responsible. It's our job to let her family attend her funeral. There's no choice. Why should I apologize for sympathizing with the boy?"

"We all sympathize. But sympathy won't bring the old woman here, especially in the middle of the winter. Don't even think of it!"

"But why not?" He flushed at the consul's bluntness. "You'll excuse me, but I didn't come all this way not to think of our government's incompetence. On the contrary. I'm here to see to it that competence prevails. I'm a human resources manager and I know what a mother's death means to a boy, even if he pretends not to care. Why shouldn't we bring his grandmother to mourn with him? If not by air, then by land . . ."

"You can forget about that, too. The trip from her village

takes several days and you can't count on transportation. She could never manage it by herself even if she wanted to. I don't understand why you're so obstinate about not burying a coffin you brought yourself."

The emissary rebuked her sharply. "First of all, *I* did not bring it. It was sent by your government and mine. I accompanied it as a gesture of goodwill. And second, the funeral can be postponed. That's not a problem. I have a document from the Central Pathology Institute. Even if I can't read it, I'm quite sure it's satisfactory."

"I swear, I don't know what you're getting at."

"What am I getting at?" It was a question he was asking himself as well. Yet the cold that was shrivelling him couldn't chill his inner zeal. "It isn't so complicated. Even if it's only a matter of making up for a clerical error, one depicted by this journalist as a nasty case of inhumanity for which I'm here to compensate this young man" – he pointed to the boy, who could tell that he was being talked about – "that's no reason to ignore his psychological distress. It's based on the genuine, and to my mind legitimate, desire that his grandmother be with him at the funeral. Why shouldn't we agree?"

"Why not, indeed? But unfortunately, this grandmother exists only in theory. Not only hasn't she heard the news yet, she's too far away to do anything about it when she does."

The resource manager felt all eyes on him – the handsome boy's and distrustful ex-husband's too. The driver had joined them as well. Even though the three of them couldn't follow the Hebrew conversation, they sensed that the emissary from a distant land was struggling with a new idea. Breath steaming from their silent mouths, the photographer and the journalist looked at the manager benevolently, curious to see how far he could push their story against the consul's practical objections.

"First of all," he said, addressing the consul with an imperious dryness, "suppose you tell me what we're talking about. How far is it to the village?"

"Do you think I know? My husband can tell you exactly. I'd say there are at least five hundred kilometres of difficult terrain between us and this boy's grandmother."

"Five hundred kilometres? That's not so bad . . . "

"Possibly more. Don't hold me to it. It could be *six*."

"Six hundred is doable, too. How long will it take? Two days at the most."

"You'll never do it in two days. Get that out of your head. You're in the wrong world again. The roads here are terrible."

"Let's say three. Even four. I'm taking this boy to his grandmother."

"And what will we do with it while you're taking him?"

"Do with what?"

"The coffin."

"We'll take it with us. There's no choice. We'll bring the woman back to the village she was born in. The boy and his grandmother will bury her there. Isn't that the right, the natural thing to do?"

"It's a noble idea!" exclaimed the weasel, who had been following the argument with interest. "It's absolutely the right thing to do."

"Will you come with us?"

"Of course." The weasel smiled. "While steering clear of you, of course."

"Yes. Do that."

The consul, however, looked askance at this unexpected proposal. The visitors from Israel did not know what kind of country they were in.

"Why look for trouble? Let's bury her here. We can bring the grandmother to the grave next summer. Our consulate has no budget for your trip."

"Don't worry. I'll pay for it. It's cheaper than a helicopter."

"Especially a nonexistent one."

Relieved at having at least shot down the helicopter, the consul turned to the ex-husband, who was anxiously awaiting an explanation. The boy and the driver listened, too. As the father frowned and shook his head in disapproval, his son slipped free of him and skipped lightly to the emissary, his face bright with excitement. Full of emotion, he leaned towards the hand of the head of personnel which he brushed lightly with his Tartar eyes before planting a grateful kiss on it. Then he straightened up: he was almost as tall as his startled benefactor. Behind him, the greenish fog through which the nearby city gleamed, was lifting. With this new warmth in his veins, the emissary felt the cold's iron grip weaken. Uncertain how to respond to the wordless gratitude of a youngster labelled a juvenile delinquent, he touched the pilot's cap and smiled in bewilderment, as the photographer popped another flash-bulb.

II

The consul was still upset. Apart from wanting her breakfast, she had counted on getting rid of the corpse that same morning. There was a small church near the cemetery in which she had planned to hold a ceremony before noon, followed by a lunch for the mourners at the government's expense; beyond that her responsibility did not extend. Now the human resources manager had made her call everything off. She urgently needed to consult her husband. If only he had been there, he might have nipped it all in the bud.

Going to the locked door of the terminal, she shook it more vigorously than would have been permitted to someone without diplomatic immunity. It was opened by a policeman, to whom she explained that a next-of-kin had been found, a young man who was prepared to claim the coffin and vouch for its burial in his mother's village. The policeman went to wake the officer – who, only too pleased to return the woman to her native soil, hurriedly put on his uniform and produced the requisite forms. Since the young man was none too adept at reading or writing, the consul helped him fill these out. Then the papers were presented to the ex-husband for his approval.

Meanwhile, the imminent arrival of another flight and its subsequent takeoff had brought the little airport back to life.

Departing travellers and welcome parties mingled noisily and the small buffet opened its doors, filling the air with cigarette smoke and the smell of coffee and pastries. With a reassuring whirr of propellers, a converted military transport touched down smoothly on the tarmac, and the policemen dusted off their uniforms and donned their caps. Soon the disembarking passengers were pushing baggage trollies through the terminal, among them – lo and behold! – the consul's husband. Smiling and spruce-looking, his steely curls piled high on his head, the freed hostage wheeled out a trolley with the leather suitcase and the two gift boxes from the bakery.

"Where's the coffin?" the worried consul asked.

"The coffin," her husband sighed, "we will have to carry out. Now that they know we're taking it, they want nothing more to do with it. I suppose it must unnerve them ... not that I'm any judge. I've never felt more peaceful than I did beside it."

"Let's first fortify ourselves with something to eat and drink," the consul said.

Her shrewd husband, however, advised otherwise. "That can wait until we get home. The coffin has to be moved before the airport shuts down again. We don't want a new officer go through the whole thing again."

He explained the task to the engineer and his son and asked the resource manager, "What do you think? There are four of us, not counting my wife. Can we manage by ourselves without the driver?"

"Why send for the driver," the emissary replied, "when the two men who got me into this predicament are standing here doing nothing?"

The journalist and the photographer good-naturedly agreed to lend a hand. Then the five adults and the boy descended to the cubicle in the basement. Resourcefully finding a way to fit the coffin through the narrow door, they started up the stairs bearing it on their shoulders, dutifully following the instructions of the consul's husband. The coffin was heavy. Having spent time with it in private, the resource manager was not alarmed by the coffin's metal edge that cut into his shoulder, although he could sense the boy's nervousness as he came into contact with it for the first time. The youngster would have lost his grip and stumbled, bringing them all down with him, had not his father pushed him out of the way.

The five of them climbed on, the consul's husband and the dead woman's ex-husband holding up the coffin's front end, the journalist and the photographer carrying the rear. In the middle, by himself, was the emissary, the human resources manager of the company that had forgotten the woman's existence. Anyone less expert than the old farmer, who directed them in two languages at once, might not have brought them safely up the stairs. They proceeded carefully, taking each step and turn with care. A sour smell accompanied them. The resource manager was not sure whether it came from the coffin or from the unwashed body of the boy, who had chosen to stick close to him and once or twice to reach out a helping hand.

"If I'm not steering clear enough of you," the weasel panted behind him, "don't complain. This was your idea . . ."

The human resources manager snorted. Unable to turn around, he could think of no rejoinder. He had to keep his eyes on the stairs, at the top of which, as they neared the exit, the light was growing brighter.

We were waving goodbye to the departing passengers when a metal coffin passed by on the shoulders of five pallbearers. We watched them carefully place it in a van and asked with a catch in our throats: Who died? Where? Where is the body being taken?

When we were told it was a local woman murdered in Jerusalem, we crossed ourselves and prayed for her eternal rest and resurrection. One of the pallbearers, a photographer, hastened to record our prayer with his camera.

12

The old van's wheels spun in the snow, then broke free. The consul and her husband sat by the driver. The coffin was in the back. On one side of it were the boy and his father – who, though relieved of all responsibility for its burial, still hoped for compensation. On the other side, more intimately than he would have liked, the resource manager sat squeezed between the weasel and the photographer. Those two still hadn't got over their good fortune in the dramatic new turn their story had taken.

The ride into town wasn't long. Even so, when the consul complained of having to miss breakfast because of her husband's impatience, the resource manager didn't hesitate. Opening a carton, he took out the bread and cake.

The baked goods took everyone by surprise, as much by their freshness as by their unexpected appearance. The hungry consul was not alone in asking for seconds. The boy wanted more, too, perhaps feeling that it brought him closer to his mother. To the distress of the resource manager, who wished to leave something for the grandmother, their appetites, sharpened by the cold, clear morning, quickly polished off the carton. At least, he thought, the old man will be delighted to know what a hit his products were. Reaching for his phone, he dialled Jerusalem despite the early hour, certain the owner would be happy to hear from him. The housekeeper, recognizing his voice and aware of his mission, reported that the master had gone to synagogue for Sabbath services and would be back soon.

"Services?" The human resources manager was astonished. "I've worked for him for over ten years and never seen an ounce of religion in him."

"What you see from up close you don't see from afar," the housekeeper answered sententiously, and offered to take a message. But the resource manager did not wish to reveal his new plan – certainly not in English – to an Indian housekeeper. He asked her to inform the owner that his products had been appreciated and promised to call again later.

The journalist, having helped to carry the coffin, had become a character in his own story and now felt entitled to ask for the use of the phone, a handy instrument if ever he had seen one. Not wishing to appear stingy, the resource manager gritted his teeth and let the weasel chatter with friends and family while the white stone buildings of the city drew nearer. How, he wondered, would his mission, of whose moral sublimity he felt more and more convinced, look in the pages of the weekly?

The weasel was still bantering over the phone as they entered the city, a provincial capital. Their first stop was the large building that housed the consulate – that is, the consul and her husband's apartment. After backing carefully into the courtyard, they unloaded the coffin, placed it in a shady corner among the garbage cans and piles of firewood, and covered it with a tarpaulin.

The time had come for their little group to split up. The emissary would ascend with the consul to her apartment. The consul's husband and the driver would go to make arrangements for the expedition to the dead woman's village – the former planned to take the letter from Central Pathology to a doctor who could tell him how long a trip the corpse might withstand; the latter had to look for snow tyres. The journalist and the photographer were to be dropped off at a small hotel and the boy left at his father's to prepare for the journey to his grandmother's. They would soon be reunited, all except for the ex-husband – who, his role ended, must now part from them all. This was more easily said than done, however: he clutched his son as if hoping to trade him for a bounty paid out by a world that had done nothing but betray him. Sensing his despondency, the human resources manager offered him the second carton as a farewell gift. "What's in it?" asked the man in surprise, reaching into his pocket for a jackknife and slitting the cardboard top. He quickly went through the pads, notebooks, and binders and feverishly ransacked the carton's bottom; then, eyes burning with humiliation, he spat and swore roundly. The consul and her husband hastened to calm him.

"What did he say? What does he want?"

The man, so it seemed, was enraged more by the affront to

his ex-wife's dignity than by any to his own. She had been an engineer, like him, with a diploma – how could the resource manager have made her stoop to the level of a cleaning woman?

"I made her?"

"In your capacity as personnel manager," the consul said.

"And what did you tell him?"

"That he should be grateful she was given a job at all and not thrown into the street when her boyfriend left her."

The resource manager shook his head. "That's not what you should have said," he declared, with a compassionate glance at the ex-husband, who was still holding on to his son. Seen in the shadows of the courtyard, the boy's exquisitely formed features made the emissary feel slightly drunk. If I'm not careful, he thought, his father won't let him come with us. The man needs encouragement. Taking out his wallet, he extracted several large bills and held them out. As the ex-husband reached for them, the photographer's camera flashed. The consul and her husband exchanged worried glances. The driver, standing to one side, turned pale. The ex-husband was speechless. Although he had hoped for more than notebooks and writing implements, he hadn't dreamed of anything like this.

"That's way too much," the consul whispered to the resource manager. "You'll spoil them."

"Never mind ... " The emissary smiled and stuffed the bills into the engineer's jacket pocket, as much to forestall any objection to his son's joining their expedition as to draw a final line between him and the dead woman. The man seemed well aware of his role in the bargain. Without even a thank-you, he took the crumpled bills, straightened them one by one, counted them silently in front of everyone, and slipped them sombrely into his wallet before murmuring a few choked words.

"What did he say?"

"That the money is his by right. Just imagine!"

"Perhaps it is," the resource manager said generously. He

laid a hand on the engineer's shoulder and patted the boy's head. "You'll use up all of your film," he warned the photographer.

"Don't worry. I brought lots more."

"He has to shoot a thousand frames," the journalist said, "to find one he likes. And that's always the one the editor rejects."

The consul's apartment, though old and small, was pleasantly domestic. Taking off her fur coat and wool cap, she went to the bedroom and returned in a colourful house robe that lent a touch of exuberance to her tall, peasantlike figure. After all the bread and cake she was still hungry, and she now went to the kitchen to prepare a late but proper breakfast for herself and her guest. Brandishing a knife as she appeared and disappeared in the kitchen doorway, she told the resource manager about the consulate as he sat sprawled on a creaky, none too steady couch. Basically, her position was honorary. When their farm in Israel failed, during the last recession, she and her husband had decided to get back on their feet by returning to their native land. To avoid the appearance of outright emigration at a time of daily terror attacks, they had proposed establishing, in exchange for the rent, an Israeli consulate that would provide services and advise the occasional tourist who came here from Israel or the even rarer local resident who wished to visit it. Now and then they also had to deal with dead bodies, which travelled in both directions.

"Dead bodies from here, sent to Israel?" The resource manager was amazed. "You mean that happens, too?"

"Of course. An Israeli mountain climber can get killed in a fall, or a hiker may freeze to death in a river. Or else someone is careless enough to be murdered in shady circumstances. This is a big, varied country. It may be poor and primitive, but it's also fabulously beautiful, especially in summer and autumn. It's a shame you had to come at this time of year ..."

The manager snorted. So did the couch beneath him. No one had asked at what time of year he would like to visit. His own desires had been irrelevant ...

"I wouldn't say that," the consul retorted, breaking egg after egg into a large frying pan as if she still had a henhouse next door. "It was you who convinced that boy – if you ask me, by the way, he's not half so innocent as you think – to bury his mother in her village. If you hadn't offered to pay the costs and go yourself, the only grandmother he would have seen this winter would have been the one in his dreams. Not that I have anything against it if you have the time and money and want to be generous. You might even cross a few frozen rivers yourself . . . Well, go and wash, then we'll eat. I'd planned to go out for a good meal after the funeral, as is the custom here, but what's done is done. You've made a mess of things."

The consul's hearty appetite infected the emissary, too. She plied him with a local aquavit, and his head spun as though he were on a ship's ladder in a stormy sea. When his conversation began to flag, the consul offered him her bed to nap in; she wouldn't hear of it when he suggested that he sleep on the creaky couch. Yes, she was tired, too, having hardly slept all night. But the emissary, who had had a long flight, came first. It was her consular duty to see that he got some rest. Once he'd closed the shutters, turned out the lights, and crawled under the blankets, Israel and its problems would seem far away. "Off with you to the bedroom, then! There's no time to lose. They've forecast a bad storm. You'll have to get an early start to stay ahead of it."

Although the resource manager had a horror of other people's double beds, he was grateful for the chance to get away from the consul's chatter and make a few telephone calls. He just didn't want her changing any sheets or pillow-cases for him. A blanket and a small pillow were all he needed. He would kick off his shoes and sleep in his clothes.

"If that's all it takes to put you to sleep, be my guest," the consul said, yielding with maternal resignation. "Just take your suitcase and bag, so that I don't end up tripping over them."

She handed him a pillow and spread the blanket while he asked whether she was coming with them.

"Absolutely not! My consular duties ended at the airport. I confirmed that the family has taken possession of the coffin and plans to bury it. Any decision to humour that boy is your affair, not the consulate's. I've done my bit. I'm just curious to know why you've got so involved. Is it guilt towards the mother – or something about the boy himself?"

"Then perhaps your husband might join us." The resource manager dodged the consul's question, feeling suddenly worried. "How will we manage with no knowledge of the language? We won't even be able to communicate with our driver ... "

"My husband is no longer a young man. He doesn't owe the government anything."

"The government has nothing to do with this. I'll pay him for his time and effort."

"You will?"

"Of course. Generously ... "

"Then that's another story."

The consul's spirits appeared to soar. Going briskly to the window, she drew the curtain, switched on a reading lamp above the bed, and shut the door behind her, urging the emissary to sleep well.

There was silence at last. But his satellite phone needed recharging. The journalist had drained the battery with his chatter. Moreover, the only electrical outlet in the room was antique and did not fit the plug, so he abandoned the idea of calling the old owner, who might finish off the battery completely with his objections to their planned trip, and dialled his mother instead. His conversations with her were always to the point. To his delight, his daughter was there too, having decided to spend the night at her grandmother's in her father's empty bed. Rather than ask her about herself, as he usually did, he told her of his experiences, describing the snow and ice and the long trip ahead of them with the orphaned boy – a nice-looking teenager, as he had expected, but highly-strung and full of anger at his mother's death. His daughter hung on every word and wanted to know more.

The unexpected conversation cheered him. But his phone was beeping a warning, so he switched it off, disconnecting himself from the world, then turned off the reading lamp, pulled up the blanket, and tried to fall asleep. On a shelf in the darkness, the glass figurines of cows, horses, chickens, and sheep, mementos of a lost farm, shone with a reddish gleam. He thought worriedly of the coffin standing by itself in the courtyard. *What a turn of events*, he mused ruefully. *A foreign woman ten years older than myself, whom I can't even remember, has become my sole responsibility. National Insurance has closed her file, her ex-husband has turned his back on her, her lover disappeared long ago, and even the consul no longer wishes to represent her. That leaves me in a cold, primitive land in the company of two journalists who think I'm a story, led by a teenage boy I'm not sure I can handle. How could I have known last Tuesday, when I promised to take this woman on my back, that she would weigh as much as she does?*

He threw off the blanket, walked to the window without switching on the light, and carefully opened the shutters in the hope of sighting the courtyard below. It took a while to spot the coffin, still beneath its tarpaulin. A crowd of curious children had gathered around it. Apparently aware, so it seemed, of what was in it, an elderly tenant was standing guard to ward them off. The resource manager felt grief for the woman, dumped like a nobody in the ugly courtyard of a strange building. Had he done the right thing by prolonging her last journey? Might it not have been wiser to have kept silent at the airport and let father and son work things out for themselves? Perhaps the boy would have given in; by now the woman would have been buried and it would all be over, the Jerusalem weekly would have its story and the old owner's humanity would be restored.

If only those Tartar eyes hadn't brushed his hand as the young lips touched it! He now had a clear notion of what the cleaning woman must have looked like. For the first time since his involvement in the affair, he felt obliged not only to see it through all the way to the end but also to *feel* it all the way, too.

He closed the shutters, returned to the consular bed, buried his face in the velvet pillow with a slight feeling of nausea, and covered himself again. It was late in the day when the loud, merry voice of the consul's returning husband woke him.

He slipped into his shoes, folded the blanket, straightened the bedcover, and entered the living room. The consul and her husband were sitting down to another meal.

"You're all set." The old farmer's blue eyes twinkled. "We've found you a good four-by-four vehicle with snow tyres for the roughest roads. The doctor and I had a look at the document you brought. It could use some literary editing, but its contents are encouraging."

"Meaning?"

"That she's been properly embalmed and is in no rush to be buried. You can travel to the ends of the earth with her. That's no cause for concern."

"Then what is?"

"The storm that's on its way."

"Your wife ..." The resource manager felt a nervous flutter. "She must have told you how much I'd like you to come with us. You can be in charge. That way I'd have a private consul of my own ..."

"He's already my private consul," said the consul affectionately, stroking her husband's silver curls.

"In a manner of speaking," the husband chuckled, planting a kiss on his wife's cheek.

"Naturally, you'd be compensated for your time and effort."

"Don't worry about that," the old farmer said. "I'd do it for nothing, out of sheer sympathy and curiosity. But if you want to pay me, why not?"

"I'll pay handsomely." The emissary was moved. "I've had faith in you from the moment I met you."

The consul smiled and put another dumpling on her husband's plate. "If you have faith in me too," she said, "you'll pull up a chair and eat some solid food. Do you hear that wind? It's getting stronger and whispering, 'It's time to get going.'"

PART THREE

The Journey

I

Tell us, you hard people: After desecrating the Holy Land and turning murder and destruction into a way of life, by what right do you now trample on our feelings? Is it because you and your enemies have learned to kill each other and yourselves with such crazy impunity, bombing and sowing endless destruction, that you think you can leave a coffin, with no explanation or permission, in the courtyard of an apartment building in someone else's country and disappear without so much as a by-your-leave?

How could you have failed to think of our children, suddenly faced, among garbage cans and gas canisters, with an anonymous death not hallowed by flowers or prayers? Didn't you think of the nightmares they might have? Of the questions they might ask us? Heartless though you are, you must know that only a clever neighbour with the wits to shield them kept their play from turning into horror.

And what were we supposed to do? How were we to protect ourselves? By calling some numskull of a policeman and bribing him to believe that we had nothing to do with it? How could we prove that a corpse that turned up one Saturday afternoon in our courtyard belonged to no one?

There was nothing to do but clench our teeth and look out of our windows until you returned. At dusk you came breezing back in an armoured vehicle from some ancient war. We recognized you at once: hardened foreigners, a race of cunning wanderers who – again without explaining yourselves – loaded the coffin onto a trailer and disappeared into the darkness. The dictators who ran our lives until recently behaved the same way.

And even afterwards, oddly enough, we felt no relief. A faint, inexplicable sorrow continued to gnaw at us. We still didn't know whose body it was or how it had died. Where had it come from? Where was it going? Our biggest grievance against you is: Why did you make off with it so quickly?

It wasn't easy for the two journalists to set out on such short notice from a small hotel in which they had made themselves at home. Yet in a winter like this they could never have managed to reach the grandmother's village on their own. Moreover, they knew that a coffin's voyage over distant steppes, undertaken at the whim of an orphaned boy, would grip their readers more than a mere grieving old woman reunited with her dead daughter.

The transportation offered them was better than they had expected, the driver having convinced the consul's husband – now promoted by the human resources manager to full acting consul – to rent, not a minibus, but a converted army-surplus personnel carrier. Square and steel-plated, it had huge wheels that kept it well off the treacherous ground; to enter it they had to use a ladder. Though its exterior was still combat grey, great pains had been taken to refashion it comfortably within. It had been stripped of its battle stations and given wide, well-upholstered seats, baggage racks, and overhead lights. Inside, all that remained of its military past were the silent green dials on its dashboard and two tripods welded to the floor. The trailer bearing the woman's coffin had no doubt once been used to transport a heavy mortar or ammunition crates.

The driver had been reinforced as well. The acting consul, who wore his wife's warm red wool cap as the badge of his promotion, had acceded to the young man's request and drawn on the emissary's generous expense account to hire a second driver, who just happened to be the first driver's elder brother. An expert navigator and mechanic, he urged the group to set out without delay and use the night time to put as much distance as possible between themselves and the approaching storm.

The resource manager, unfamiliar with local prices, had no idea what all this would cost. Yet the fact that the pittance he had paid the embittered ex-husband had sufficed to make the man drop all complaints encouraged him to think that in this case, too, the expense would not be great. For a reasonable sum he would restore the owner's humanity, which had been maligned by the journalist who now joined the photographer in admiring the converted carrier.

"But where's the child?" the resource manager asked

anxiously, concerned that the handsome youngster might have vanished at the last moment.

"Child?" The new consul objected to the term. "Is that what you take him for? Wait till you see where we're about to pick him up. You can tell me then whether you think he's a child . . ."

The city's streets were broad and deserted. There were few pedestrians and the shops were closed, because of the night or, perhaps, the storm. The high-placed headlights of the vehicle were reflected by the stairways and entrances of monumental buildings decorated with turrets and spires and guarded by bearded sentinels in sheepskin coats. A group of middle-aged, snugly wrapped women with shopping baskets stood silently on a corner, awaiting transportation back to their village.

On the outskirts of town, the party entered a parking lot. It belonged to an abandoned factory, beside which piles of un-identifiable raw materials lay rotting. A loudspeaker attached to a tall chimney blasted earsplitting disco music. The power-fully built mechanic, doubting the consul's competence in such matters, went inside and emerged a few minutes later with the delicately built boy in tow. The young man's face had an alcoholic flush; he carried a small backpack and was dressed in the same pilot's hat and overalls he'd worn that morning. They seated him in the back among the bags and suitcases and told him to keep an eye on his mother's coffin, which, though firmly connected to the trailer, might be jolted loose.

The boy glanced with wonder at the vehicle, pleased at having brought so elaborate a scheme into being. He still had the same sour smell. The weasel made a face. "Gentlemen," he murmured, "if we don't make this young Adonis take a bath at our first stop, we'll have to cease breathing." The emissary saw the boy redden. We have to be careful, he thought. He must still know some Hebrew from his time spent in Jerusalem. "*Shalom*," he said, giving the youngster a friendly smile to make him feel at ease. "I'll bet," he added, "that's one word you still remember." Yet the boy only grew redder and said nothing, and cast his handsome eyes glumly downwards as if even one word from the city that had killed his mother was too much for him. Slowly he turned to look behind him, as much at the first dark signs of the storm, which was now blotting out the fading city on the horizon, as at the coffin bobbing up and down in the reddish glare of the taillights.

From the outset, the older driver took the younger one, who seemed glad to yield to his authority, under his wing. It was clear that he would decide on their route, which he did by choosing a longer one with better and more-travelled roads. Once assured that his brother had mastered the controls, he turned his attention to the decommissioned dials on the dashboard, determined to put them back in working order. The consul, having had experience with machinery as a farmer, joined in the effort and soon brought a dial back to life; although its purpose remained a mystery, its steady flicker cheered them all. Although the vehicle handled roughly and noisily, its gears letting out a double groan when shifted and its huge wheels jouncing for no apparent reason, they felt they had embarked safely on a real adventure. Not even the yellow gleam of the distant storm in the rearview mirror, which the mechanic pointed out as if he were a radiologist reading a worrisome X-ray, could dampen their spirits.

The darkness thickened. The road, though otherwise a relatively good one, was full of potholes. The emissary, turning to glance at the boy whose handsome face was now invisible, saw that the journalist had switched on his light and was making notes.

"If not for that smear job of yours," he said without anger, "I'd be in a warm bed now instead of bouncing around in the cold."

"In bed? So early?" The journalist smiled and shut his notebook. "That's a bit of a stretch. It's eight p.m. here, which means the Sabbath has just ended in Jerusalem. From what I know, that's your bar time, not your bedtime."

"You even trailed me to the bars?"

"I didn't. He did." He pointed to the photographer. "He needed a picture."

"He should have taken a better one."

"What's wrong with the one he took? It's realistic."

"Look who's talking about reality," snarled the human resources manager.

"I believe in it and aim for it. Why should you care about your picture in the paper? No one will think more or less of you because of it. Only your actions will determine that. To tell the truth, I'm beginning to think more of you myself."

"You are? I'm honoured!" The resource manager was sarcastic. "Finally, I stand a chance with you. Just what is it you think so much of, may I ask?"

"Your ability to discern the plot of this story."

"Which is?"

"Bringing this cleaning woman to a grave in her native village. That's the kind of humanity I feel proud of. I feel proud of my own too, of course."

"Just a minute. What does your humanity have to do with this?"

"Whose if not mine? Don't dismiss what I've done this time. Over the years I've written dozens of angry articles. I've attacked people and institutions. Until now, I never accomplished a thing. The libel suits I was threatened with may have been dropped, but those who threatened me went on looking right through me. They read what I wrote and said, 'No comment.'"

"That's what I told the owner to say, too."

"It's to his credit that he didn't listen to you. This is the first time an article of mine, dashed off late at night, has changed anything. It led not only to an admission of guilt from a large bakery, but to action. Believe me, that's made me an optimist again. An idea born in my brain has us all headed for the ends of the earth in an armoured vehicle. You must admit that for a weasel, that's not bad ... By the way, take a look at these tripods. You're an ex-military man – what do you think they were for? They must be from the First World War. You'll see, my friend! You'll see what I make of all this! The editor has promised me a third of the issue if I bring him a story with some punch ... "

"I hope you'll at least acknowledge that it's courtesy of the company you slandered."

The weasel laughed good-naturedly.

"I may – and then again, I may not. So what if all this was paid for by a company that will only increase its profits as a result?"

"I thought you took pride in being objective."

"Objectivity is a point of view. If you have it, nothing can destroy it. I'm here to report on how a businessman came to regret the callousness with which his company treated its workers and decided on a goodwill gesture of atonement. But since he also knows that if the gesture isn't publicized it hasn't happened, he's saddled you with a photographer and a journalist to make sure his atonement is remembered on earth as well as in heaven. And with my help it will be, because I'll write that there are still decent men in this depraved world who can accept legitimate criticism. You yourself are not only a private individual in my story, you're a symbol. An aloof executive, a former army officer oblivious of the fact that a cleaning woman killed by terrorists went on collecting her pay packet, is now on his way to do penance, braving a winter storm on an expedition to a far land where he will beg forgiveness on bended knee."

"Hey, go easy ... " The human resources manager laughed. "If you don't watch it you'll end up on bended knee yourself, with your photographer taking a picture."

"Now that's an idea!" The journalist liked it. "If I can fit it into the story – why not? We'll lift the lid of the coffin and give our readers a glimpse of death itself. An artistic one, shot with a zoom lens from a distance ... "

"Don't you dare!"

"What's wrong now?"

"I'm warning you!" The resource manager's amusement had turned to anger. "Don't you dare think of opening the coffin ... do you hear me?"

"But why get worked up? I beg to remind you that having that woman on your payroll doesn't make her your personal property ... Perhaps you've forgotten, but you're here as an escort, just like me. If she belongs to anyone, it's to her son. He signed for her and he'll decide. Suppose the grandmother wants to open the coffin for a farewell look, who'll stop her? With all due respect to your expense account, you're not the boss here."

Anger was now becoming feverish hatred.

"I'm warning you! Don't you dare! Don't print more crap in that goddamn newspaper of yours!"

"But why get worked up? What's the paper to you? Do you ever read it?"

"Never. The first thing I do on Friday morning is toss it out without opening it."

"There you are! So what do you care what's in it? Not that you aren't missing things, believe me. Precisely because we know that most of our readers aren't interested in local news and only look at the rentals and used-car ads, we sometimes run surprising features, good investigative reporting on little-known subjects."

"I believe I'll go right on missing them."

"That's your right. Just hand me that satellite phone of yours, if you don't mind. I want to know if my son is back from his school hike."

"I'm not handing you anything. You've already drained my battery with all your talk. The consul had no outlet to recharge it. There are more important things than your son's hike. I've told you: you're here strictly as an accessory. I was generous enough to let you and your photographer tag after me, but that's over with now. From now on you'll keep your distance, is that clear?"

The weasel winced in the circle of his reading light. For the first time the emissary felt that he had managed to hurt this pudgy fellow, on whose unshaven chin a thin strip of beard had appeared.

A heavy silence descended on the vehicle. From afar, its big wheels and high-set lights made it look like a hovering spaceship. The boy had disappeared among the bags and suitcases, his long limbs folded into them. The human resources manager, weary and dejected, turned his back on the journalist, spread out his legs, and hung his scarf on a tripod. The consul removed his wife's red cap; his steel-grey curls blew in the wind. The resource manager kept his eyes on the green dials until he dozed off to the sound of the powerful engine.

2

The engine's silence woke him. He opened his eyes and found himself deserted. The other passengers were stretching their limbs outside, at a junction with road signs. It was nearly midnight. He stepped outside, and was surprised to see that the starry sky was bright and clear despite the biting cold. They had stayed ahead of the storm, and the two brothers, conversing quietly while one lit a cigarette from the glowing tip of the other's, had reason to feel pleased as they affectionately kicked the vehicle's big wheels. The consul, waving hello with a snowy branch, was in a good mood, too. He was observing the photographer, who had taken advantage of the break to shoot the vehicle from every angle. The boy, blue with cold but wide awake, was copying the Cyrillic letters of the road signs into the journalist's notebook.

It was 10 p.m. in Jerusalem. The Sabbath was long over. Now was a good time to report on his progress to the owner. Even if the old man thought their journey unnecessary, or downright dangerous, there was nothing he could do about it now. The human resources manager could without fear inform him of the latest developments. Looking for a quiet spot, he found one to the rear of the trailer, the high-set wheels of which raised the coffin to eye level. A white rime had formed a strange crust on it, like crocodile scales, the result of its rapid passage through the frigid air. He tried peeling off a scale and stopped when the cold burned his fingers.

He opened his satellite phone and extended the antenna. But all the stars in the sky, as close and friendly as they looked, could not put him through to Jerusalem. The weasel had talked the battery to death. Cursing him under his breath, the resource manager shifted his position, but to no avail. The consul, seeing his frustration, came over to offer encouragement.

"Don't worry. We'll find a solution for your battery."

"If you don't," the resource manager said disconsolately, "we'll be cut off from the world."

"No chance of that!" Perched on his grey hair, the red woollen cap lent the old optimist a childlike charm. "We may even have it already. You may not have noticed, but these two daredevils managed to push this monster nearly a third of the distance while we slept. Instead of continuing fifty kilometres to a dosshouse in the next town, they'd like your permission to make a slight detour."

"What kind of detour?"

"A minor one. They propose changing course from east to north, twenty or thirty kilometres to a small valley where there's an army base. During the Cold War it was a top-secret installation. Now it's a tourist site."

The consul explained that as relations between the two superpowers had thawed, so that threats of war no longer accompanied hopes for peace, the economic situation had surprisingly – or perhaps predictably – deteriorated. Bloated military budgets had been drastically cut. Entire army units, especially in outlying areas, found themselves on the verge of starvation, forced to survive not only by selling or renting old equipment like this armoured vehicle, but also by opening country inns and restaurants on their bases. In a former nuclear command post in the valley to the north, dug out in the 1950s, there was now a museum, half historical and half technological, that showed visitors – for an entrance fee, of course – how the country's leaders had planned to survive a nuclear war.

"And that's worth making a detour for?"

"A minor one. Twenty or thirty kilometres in each direction. The drivers have heard of it and would like to visit it, and agreeing will ensure a pleasant continuation of our trip. Besides, they say there is good accommodation there and first-rate food. And there's a tour of the operation rooms, complete with a simulation of all planned first strikes, counterstrikes, and counter-counterstrikes. It's an interactive exhibition that demonstrates the catastrophe that the pressing of a single button could have loosed upon the world."

"Computer games!"

"Yes and no. A game replayed on its original field with the original ball is more than virtual. And we're in no hurry. The roads are better than we anticipated and the old woman may not have returned to her village yet. Why sit waiting for her in the middle of nowhere when we can enjoy The War That Never Was? Just because we've set out on a hard, sad winter's journey doesn't mean we have to be obsessive about it. Why not have some educational fun? As far as she's concerned" – he inclined his silver curls towards the coffin – "there's no need to worry. My private doctor has assured me on the basis of your document that we're in no rush to bury her. You can see for yourself that she's well-refrigerated."

The consul's matter-of-fact argument drew the attention of the two drivers, who now approached them with the apprehensive boy, whose wide-eyed gaze lingered on the frost-covered coffin. Now close enough to inhale his steamy breath, the human resources manager could see that he wasn't the clone of his mother, though he felt sure the boy was the clue to her beauty, which had once eluded him.

The journalist stood off to one side, at a distance from the photographer, who was now preparing to snap a nocturnal portrait of the group around the coffin. He was finally, it seemed, taking the resource manager's warning seriously. By the icy light of the flickering stars, the resource manager had a sudden memory. Yes, he did recall someone who had looked like the journalist, though considerably thinner, from his year at university.

"All right," he ruled indulgently. "We'll take the detour and have our doomsday fun – but on one condition. Twenty-four hours will be the most we spend on it, not a minute more."

"Not a minute more," the consul promised happily. "And I guarantee that you'll find an outlet there for your charger."

When the consul translated the decision into the local language, everyone was satisfied, even the motherless boy who had no reason to hasten his mother's burial. They clambered back into the armoured vehicle, and the engine roared a hearty thank-you. The journalist and the boy exchanged the hint of a smile, and the human resources manager wondered whether some new, wordless alliance had sprung up between them that would help the weasel stage a dramatic climax to his story? Afraid that things might get out of hand, he decided on a change of tone. Turning to the seat behind him, he declared:

"You know, I now realize why I didn't remember you. Back then, at university, you were thinner and even more weaselly . . ."

The surprised journalist laughed, then let out a sigh.

"Don't remind me of how thin I was. Those days are gone forever. But you haven't changed at all – and I don't mean just your looks. You still carry a shell on your back, ducking into it when anything touches you . . . though at least you now admit what I told you over the telephone. We actually did take several philosophy courses together. Not that I remember you because of anything particularly clever or foolish that you said. It's because of a gorgeous girl. Don't ask me why, but she kept coming on to you."

"Yes. I remember."

"Who was she? What happened to her?"

"What do you care? I suppose you'd like to put her into your story, too. Maybe your photographer can follow her around at night."

"There, there! You needn't be so offended. I was asking as an interested citizen, not a reporter . . ."

"When do you ever stop being a reporter? I'll bet you look

for scoops in your dreams."

"That's putting it a bit strongly. But if it's what you think, I must have really upset you. Listen, let's make up. Honestly. I'd like to offer you an apology . . . an official one . . ."

The emissary was taken aback. For a moment he shut his eyes and bowed his head.

"But tell me," the weasel asked, his natural curiosity again getting the better of him, "where did you disappear to? Did you drop out after your freshman year or just switch majors?"

"I re-enlisted in the army."

"In what branch? Manpower?

"Of course not. I was second-in-command of a combat battalion."

"With what rank?"

"Major."

"That's all? You should have stuck it out longer. Don't you know that in the Israeli army you can tie any major to a tree and come back ten years later to find that he's a colonel?"

"I guess I didn't find the right tree."

"Still. What made you leave the army?"

"I was too much of an individualist. Large organizations don't suit me."

"Then why not something more intimate . . . a small commando force of your own, for example?"

"What for? To be the dead hero of one of your articles?"

"We're back to my articles! I beg you to believe that I have other things in life."

"So I've heard. I'm told you've been working forever on a doctorate."

"Ah!" The weasel blushed. "I see you do come out of your shell sometimes."

"Apparently. But what's your subject? Why has it taken you so long?"

"Do you really want to know?"

"Do we have anything better to talk about?"

"I'm writing on Plato."

"What's left to say about him?"

"With such a complex philosopher, anyone with a little patience and common sense can always find a new angle," the journalist said, and added dourly, "not that that's why my dissertation is stuck. Our wretched reality simply keeps distracting me from it."

"Reality is only an excuse."

"You're right."

"What is it about?"

"You're sure you want to know? Or are you just trying to pass the time?"

"That too. But I'm curious to know how your mind works. I don't want to be surprised by you again."

The journalist let out a lively laugh. "It's you who are surprising. Like yesterday, for instance, when you suggested this trip, or just now, when you agreed to a detour."

"Well, I suppose I can be unpredictable, too." The human resources manager liked the idea. "But you're avoiding my question. What is your dissertation about? A specific Platonic dialogue or something more general?"

"A specific dialogue."

"Which?"

"You wouldn't recognize the name. It's one you've never heard of and never will."

"Is it one of those we discussed in our course?"

"It's *Phaedo*."

"*Phaedo*? No, I don't remember it ... unless ... "

"It's on the immortality of the soul."

"No, that's not the one I'm thinking of. There was another ... you know the one. The famous one, the one about love ... "

"If you're thinking of *The Symposium*, alias *The Banquet* – no, there really are no angles left there. Platonic love has been mined to exhaustion."

But the resource manager persisted. A friendly intellectual conversation, he thought, if not too personal, would help keep the journalist on his best behaviour. He himself remembered little of the famous Platonic dialogue, only that he had been favourably impressed that love could be discussed so candidly in a philosophy course. All that remained with him of the text itself was a story or parable about a man (but who? Adam? Everyman?) who was cut or divided in two (mistakenly? accidentally? deliberately?). Hence the human desire to reunite with one's missing half, also known as love . . .

The consul, listening from the front seat, doffed his red woollen cap and remarked:

"Even a peasant like myself knows that story. Whenever I slice an apple I feel its halves wanting to reunite. That's why I keep slicing them into smaller and smaller pieces . . . "

The human resources manager guffawed. His inner tension easing, he listened affably to the weasel's rebuke:

"That's the most superficial and obvious aspect of *The Symposium*. It's no wonder that people like you always remember it. But for such a simplistic metaphor there was no need for Socrates and his friends to gather in Agathon's house. Nor would their conversation have gone on enchanting us for thousands of years. Its real point is more profound."

"Tell us." Both the consul and the emissary were eager to know.

"Are you really in the mood now, in the middle of the night?"

"We have nothing better to do."

And so, while they sat in the dark cavern of the armoured vehicle with the two drivers in front bathed in the luminous green glow of its haphazardly working dials, the journalist strove to expound the essence of love, his voice rising above the roar of the engine as the vehicle laboured up a steep winding road. *Had I known that this detour would involve such precipitous climbs*, the human resources manager thought, *I would never have agreed to it.*

"Love," declared the weasel in high Platonic style, "bears witness to our finiteness, but also to our ability to transcend it."

Human desire ascends by rungs like those of a ladder from love's lowest manifestations to its highest, from its most concrete to its most abstract, from its most physical to its most spiritual. To have the world of true form revealed to one is the reward of the wise lover – who, freed of the physical object of his desire, realizes that his pursuit is of something more essential. The more he searches for it, the more he realizes that the ultimate beauty lies not in the body but in the soul . . .

"The soul . . . " The consul, perhaps reminded of his soulful wife, roused himself.

"That's love's secret," the weasel continued as the vehicle slowed to take the hairpin bends. "There is no formula. Each person has to find the secret for himself. That's why Eros is neither god nor man. He's a *daimon*, thick-skinned, unwashed, barefoot, homeless, and poor – yet he links the human to the divine, the temporal to the eternal . . . "

The vehicle came to a halt on the steep gradient. Worried that the trailer might break free on the long climb, the elder brother went to check the tow-bar. The sudden stop woke the boy who turned from his place amid the luggage to glance quickly back at the trailer, now awash in the beam of a torch held by the resourceful technician. Soft snowflakes danced in the bright light as he circled the coffin worriedly, examining its ropes and knots. Even this did not put his mind to rest; re-entering the vehicle, he took the wheel from his brother, trusting only in his own sure touch.

"That's also why Socrates, though he did not reject the young Alcibiades' love, also did not agree to its consummation."

"How's that?"

"True love requires separation. Plato specifies that the desired union of the two halves that so appeals to your imaginations must never take place. The love of beauty must remain open-ended. Therefore, it's always in a state of disequilibrium. Its extremes can drive a man to the most shameless acts."

3

From the first officer of the night watch to the second officer:

You're punctual, sergeant. It's time for the changing of the guard. But I'm not going to bed. I'll stay up to keep you company. Half an hour ago I would have said things seemed quiet and peaceful; the hours of sentry duty had gone by in their usual drowsy haze. But suddenly I saw something new. I won't waste words describing it. Here, take these binoculars and look out, into the darkness. Do you see that large, glowing body descending towards us through the fog? What is it? An old spacecraft re-entering the atmosphere? A UFO from a distant planet? Or am I just seeing things, as my troops always claimed? Use your fresh, young eyes, sergeant, and tell me what's out there. Should we wake the CO or wait to get a closer look? I don't want to end up a laughingstock.

I've been serving this country for over fifty years. The best years of my life have been spent right here. But the wild swings from military to civilian existence have left me depressed. I don't know what I am any more. Who can believe that a huge, state-of-the-art installation, dug into the ground in top secrecy, one of the most closely guarded bases in our vast and powerful land, is now a tourist site run by a small, undisciplined garrison?

Do you have any idea, my young friend, just how deep the nuclear shelter beneath us is? Would you believe that once upon a time an infernal elevator burrowed ten floors into the ground before it hit a false bottom? Do you realize that underneath the command rooms and storerooms are comfortable apartments, equipped for our politicians and generals to stay in with their families? That at a depth of dozens of metres are double beds for lovers, tables set for banquets, an ultramodern kitchen with an enormous freezer filled with every delicacy – all to add variety and spice to long months of hiding from radioactive poisons? Has anyone told you about the library of great books, the playrooms and games for children? There's even a hospital with maternity wards and operating theatres.

They say the threat of nuclear destruction has passed. Our former enemies are now our friends and the doomsday weapons are rotting in their silos. The pinpricks of terrorists and suicide bombers don't call for

*underground cities. And that, young man, has spelled the end of a
career soldier's world. I, who once served in war's inner sanctum, have
become a butler and a lackey. In the old command rooms, in which
every drill made history's heart skip a beat, I entertain the tourists
with Disneywars.*

*You tell me, young man: Is it so? Is peace here to stay? Can we be
so sure that a new threat – now, today, tonight – won't send us back
into hiding?*

*After all, even if we trust your twenty-twenty vision, you can't
deny there's something worrying about an unfamiliar armoured vehicle
approaching the gate with its lights raking over us, especially when it
has a coffin in tow. That's a bad omen for an ageing sergeant whom
nobody needs anymore.*

The "minor detour" to the newly opened tourist site in an
old and still partially functioning military base turned out to be
a difficult two-hour journey, climbing precipitously and then
dropping just as fast. Perhaps this was why, when stopped at
the gate by a beetle-browed veteran sergeant with a mouth
full of gold teeth, who insisted that security regulations
forbade the entry of unidentified military vehicles, the tired
drivers put up no resistance and left their vehicle outside,
instructing their passengers to take their personal belongings
and follow the old warrior several hundred metres to their
lodgings. Leaving the coffin on its trailer, they let themselves
be led, not to the guesthouse, which was half a floor underground, but to the barracks room, where three soldiers lay
asleep by a crackling stove. The sergeant handed them
blankets, pointed to some mattresses stacked against a wall,
and suggested they get some sleep; the reception officer
would register them properly in the morning.

The elderly consul, by now exhausted, took a mattress,
dragged it to a corner, pulled off his coat and shoes, and
collapsed, taking a last rueful look at his disappointing detour
before covering his head with an army blanket. The human
resources manager said nothing. His military experience had
taught him that a stern silence was the best tactic when his
troops were aware of a blunder. Choosing a mattress, he

added two blankets to the one he'd been given and lay down in the corner opposite the consul's. The two brothers chose the third corner, where they nested side by side; the fourth corner was claimed by the journalist. In high spirits after his well-received homily on love, he invited the photographer to join him and even to take his picture in commemoration of the day's trek before he bundled up and turned his head to the wall.

The boy alone took his time finding a place. After standing pensively in the middle of the room in his pilot's cap, as if looking for something he had lost, he knelt by the stove and tossed a few scattered coals into the fire. He had slept most of the way and did not seem tired now. When the old sergeant arrived with a pail of hot tea, he helped pour it into cups and hand it out to the travellers.

The human resources manager, having learned the local word for *thank you* from the consul, murmured it when the boy bashfully offered him a carefully held cup of steaming tea. The boy smiled at him, his delicate, coal-smudged fingers grazing the manager's own. The sweet beverage hit the spot. He would have liked a second cup, but the sergeant had already taken away the pail. There was nothing left to do but signal the boy to turn out the lights.

"What is this? Boot camp all over again?"

The giggly voice from under the blanket was the weasel's. The resource manager, knowing that he would have trouble falling asleep and that any banter would only make it worse, shut his eyes. At once his ears were assailed by the snoring of the consul, whose saw strokes were answered by those of a sleeping soldier.

It was 2.30 a.m. As if mesmerized by the flames that illuminated his perfect features, the boy went on crouching by the stove. Now that the others were asleep, the emissary could look at him more closely. Though he knew that the boy was aware of his gaze, he could not take his eyes off him. It's all because of his mother, he thought. I wouldn't look at her in the morgue and now I can't stop looking at her reflection.

He was not the only one. The old sergeant, too, could not sleep. Returning, ostensibly to add coals to the stove, he was soon questioning the youngster and listening to his version of their strange expedition. The conversation took place in low tones, and the human resources manager followed it by watching the boy's gestures and the white-haired sergeant's expression. Like others of his age, the sergeant inspired the resource manager's confidence and trust; he even made him miss the grand old man himself, the company owner. Recollecting that he had been out of touch with him for nearly a day, he rose from his mattress and displayed the satellite phone and its charger to the talking pair, miming the empty battery and notching two fingers for an outlet.

The surprised sergeant took the instrument and held it in his palm while consulting the boy to make sure he had understood. Undaunted by such a challenge in the middle of the night, he seemed pleased to have found a task worthy of him. Without further ado, he stuck the phone and charger into a pocket of his greatcoat and went off.

For a moment, the human resources manager was alarmed. But before he could call the sergeant back, the boy laughingly reassured him in his own language. He smiled back, patting the blond head and returning to the blankets in his corner. The boy, too, appeared to think that it was time to sleep, for he took a mattress and stood debating where to put it. After a while, as if declaring his faith in the man who had approved his mother's last journey, he set the mattress down beside him, pulled off his shoes, and began removing his overalls. Not only did he not mind the cold, he seemed to enjoy braving it. The resource manager, who had first noticed this at the airport, was not surprised when the boy stripped off his underwear in the heated room and knelt pale-skinned, smelling of stale sweat, to spread a blanket.

The human resources manager had a teenage daughter and had always been careful to avoid seeing her or her friends in the nude. Not since his high school days had he been in the presence of a naked adolescent, let alone one so ambiguous, half child and half adult, so masculine and yet also feminine. The boy had sloping shoulders and delicate feet, and his golden pubic hair had yet to declare itself. Even in the darkness his supple torso, extending from the bare buttocks, could not hide the signs, both recent and old, of scratches and actual bites, fingerprints of the delinquency the consul suspected him of. It was a suspicion confirmed by the look on his face, at once arrogant and desperate. The resource manager wondered if his nakedness was an extortion of payment, not only for his forgotten mother but also for the entire false promise of Jerusalem.

The boy got under the covers slowly, as if reluctant to part from his own naked form. His face was turned towards the man he had chosen to sleep beside. A breath away from him, the resource manager now had a close-up of the eyes that slanted upward from the bridge of a flattened nose. Confident that even the mother's magic in this boy who so moved him could not shake an inner resolve that had never failed him before, he looked away to avoid misunderstanding and said "goodnight" in Hebrew.

The boy, as if he were determined to expunge from his soul every last word of the language of the country that had killed his mother, merely smiled remotely and languidly shut his eyes. I know you're just pretending, thought the resource manager. Good night, then, and sweet dreams.

He turned to the wall, over which the flame from the stove cast its shadows until sleep snuffed them out.

For us, though, the flame goes on burning. It entices us, whirls and spins us through space and time, dream-bearers for a man in his late thirties, an ex-army officer, a divorced father of a teenage girl, a personnel manager charged with a unique mission, who now, at the first stop of his journey, in the barracks of a once-secret military base that has become a draw for tourists, lies on a thin mattress, wrapped in a foreign army blanket. Although we feel his urge to dream a dream, is it possible, in all his weariness, with the steady rasping of the sleepers around him, to give him one that will be meaningful – one that he will remember and even describe to others?

That's our job. We, the agents of the imagination, brokers of phantasms, are here to produce a dread and marvellous dream. Already we hover above shut eyelids, slip into the rhythms of the breath, stir forgotten childhood wishes into the remnants of yesterday, blend anxieties with fabulous desires, mix jealousies with memories and longings. Microscopic and transparently elusive, we pass, tiny dream nematodes, compactions of dissimulation, through the tough outer membranes of the soul.

And although we are all here for the same purpose, none of us knows any of the others. Incessantly we change our disguises. Two old childhood friends merge into a single youth. A conscript killed by a stray bullet returns as a company sergeant. The former foreign minister, now a next-door neighbour and possibly a cousin, is in attendance, too. And there are others, total strangers with no identifying marks, like a woman our souls go out to as she passes in the street.

It's twitching into life, this dream of ours. The eyelids flutter as the opening scene appears. A sigh is stifled. A leg shoots nervously out from under the blanket, followed by the other moving more slowly, as if someone were taking a first step, or, better yet, beginning a descent.

Good luck.

4

At first the dream descends broad, smooth steps. He is back home, visiting a new building on a street near his mother's in which he has rented a small, attractive apartment that will soon be available. Yet it is so easy to skip down the well-lit staircase that he has missed the prominent exit on the ground floor and gone on descending, at first without noticing that the light is growing dimmer. The steps, too, have changed and are narrower. There are no more apartments. He is exploring some sort of basement. Nor is he alone on the staircase. Old men in fur hats and long, heavy winter coats stride beside him, sighing and muttering. Well, then, the dreamer thinks excitedly, I must be in the nuclear shelter and this must be the tour. But where is the tour guide to show me round?

Now, however, the dream takes a more sombre turn. The

163

tourist site has become a frightening reality. The old men in long coats and fur hats are commissars and secret agents who have hastily launched a first strike and are hurrying to take cover from an imminent counterattack.

The steps are now narrow and steep, the walls around them crooked and constricting. In the depths of the new building stands the bell tower of an ancient church. Although he is a stranger who does not belong in this place, the dreamer wishes to be saved like all the others. Awkwardly pretending to be someone else, he is jostled into the shelter, a small, suffocating chamber filled with people casting angry, desperate glances at a transparent partition – behind which, on a small stage, bustle the leaders who have so flippantly given the dreadful order. Seen through the partition they have the silhouettes of grizzly bears oblivious to the idiocy of their actions; even so, the dreamer thinks he knows them and has run afoul of them in the past – particularly one of them, a blubbery man whose broad chest is covered with medals that look like tongues of blood and flame.

Can this be the whole secret shelter? Its entire legendary depth? Can I have agreed to make a detour here instead of proceeding straight to the village, or to take part in a war of annihilation that has nothing to do with me and that I don't deserve? Who can survive in a pitiful shelter like this? The enemy, gnashing his teeth amid the havoc we have wreaked, is launching his revenge. It will be terrible. The forked glitter of his counterstrike, it is said, can already be seen. Why stay in an indefensible place that will only draw withering fire? My place was always in the West. Why be killed by it now?

But it is already too late. The counterstrike lands on the building in utter silence. A foul, horrid, asphyxiating smell spreads through the shelter, which is also a gymnasium. Wooden ladders hang on its walls. The panicky leaders scale them to reach a high, narrow window, through which the green tip of a cypress tree is visible. The dreamer remembers the tree from his childhood, though he has never before yearned for it as he does now.

Is it still the same dream? With no interruption other than a turning of his head, a torrid sun now melts a sky of blue. It is the eve of the holiday of Shavuot, the day of the giving of the Law, and schoolchildren with wreaths of flowers on their heads pour through an open gate, racing to show their parents the little Torah scrolls they have made in class.

For whom is he waiting? He has no wife, his daughter is unborn, and no child with a wreath is looking for him. Though grown up, he is a student himself and late for class. Easing out of the rope that ties him to a tree, he flies through the blossoming garden of his old high school, over the stone footbridge that crosses a pond, and up the stairs of the school, flight after flight, until he reaches the classroom. It is deserted.

Has she cancelled the lesson, or have his fellow students skipped the class?

There is no message on the blackboard. On the teacher's chair is a slide rule brought from her native land. In spite of the holiday, then, she came for their trigonometry lesson, only to be let down by his classmates. He knows that his lateness has made him a traitor too, and so he takes the slide rule, which is warm from the sunshine, hoping that bringing it to her will gain him forgiveness. But the teachers' room is empty. The foreign trigonometry teacher has been summoned to the principal's office to be fired. Though only a student, he is certain his love and devotion can save her. And the school secretary is on his side. "Run!" she says. "They're doing it right now."

He runs and is seized by a sweet dread when he sees her by the large window in the dimly lit principal's office, slumped in an executive armchair in which she has been placed to ease the shock. He now realizes he has always known she is not a cleaning woman but a teacher. Gone are her apron, broom, and cap. She is wearing a flowery, childish summer blouse like the nightgown spread out to dry by the old owner in the shack. The collar is open, revealing a long, strong neck tilted sensuously back and perfect, sloping shoulders of white marble in which there is not a drop of blood.

The dream turns sultry with a passion he has never felt before. Is the bomber on his way to the market? Has the bomb already gone off? He is reminded that he has written down the story, not only of her life, but also of her love for him, which took place long ago when he was a child or perhaps even an infant. They made love as she nursed him. How frightful that not even so ancient a passion can save her! He leans towards the armchair to make certain there is no mistake and that this is indeed the forgotten woman the night shift supervisor was smitten by. Miryam, Miryam, he says, recalling the new, secret Hebrew name on her door. Her photograph, which he displays to others to establish her beauty, excites him. Too distraught to remember that he is only a student, he brandishes the slide rule at the principal and his assistants, who are struggling to extricate the half-dead woman from the armchair and throw her away with the rubbish.

Wait, the dreamer shouts as he runs forward, spurred by the secretary's sympathy. Give me time. A lonely but ambitious student, he embraces his teacher with a sob as though she were a fellow classmate, even though she is ten years older than he . . .

Is he still talking in his dream, or is this a thought that has spiralled out of it? For as he covers her with his kisses, he murmurs or thinks:

"Why give in? Why give up? Is there anywhere in the world a cross worth my dying on?"

5

The emissary's dream sent such pleasurable shock waves through him that he sat up the moment he opened his eyes, as though to secure the vision in his consciousness and prevent further dreams from uprooting it. Having taught himself in the army to form a mental picture of his unit the instant he awoke, making certain all his men were at their posts, he was aware of the barracks at once. A professional glance informed him that the three soldiers sleeping by the stove were gone, their place taken by three others wrapped in the same blankets.

The travellers were scattered in their corners, fast asleep. The stove, to which coal must have been added, burned brightly. Although it was still dark out, he deemed it best to have a look at the coffin. Taking care not to waken the boy, who had thrown off his blanket, he rose from the mattress. For a second he debated whether he was entitled, or perhaps even obliged, to cover the sleeping youth. Yet it seemed best not to touch him even in passing.

He dressed carefully, wrapping his scarf around his neck and slipping into his heavy winter coat before tiptoeing out with his army boots in his hands. Exchanging a quick glance with the consul, who opened bloodshot eyes, he stepped into the corridor. There the old sergeant was sleeping by a makeshift barrier erected to keep the unexpected visitors from touring the site without payment.

The resource manager had experience with sleeping sentries and had disarmed and court-martialled more than one of them. Since this was not the approach he wished to take with the wrinkled old sergeant, however, he sat down beside him and put on his boots while waiting to be noticed. Indeed the sergeant soon opened his eyes and recognized him. The boots, even if issued by another army, aroused his comradely instincts. Lifting a thin blanket, which at first glance seemed designed to warm a cat or lap dog, he revealed the satellite phone standing upright in its charger, from which improvised wires ran to a large battery that had once belonged to a half-track or tank.

Deprived of words, the resource manager could only bow an appreciative head.

The sergeant carefully detached the wires, cleaned the phone with a corner of his coat, and handed it to its owner, who immediately put it to the test by dialling his office. Within seconds he heard his own voice asking, deep in the Jerusalem night, to leave a message. Graciously complying with his own request, he reported positively on the latest developments while smiling at the sergeant's efforts to follow his conversation with himself. Yet when he took some money from his wallet and held it out, it was firmly rejected. How could an old soldier accept payment for a military duty?

Once he had assured himself that the phone was working again, the manager signalled that he wished to go outside. To allay suspicion, he mimed his intention to do no more than check the coffin. This was not easily accomplished, since the sergeant had forgotten the coffin's existence. When a rectangular box sketched in the air failed to remind him of it, the manager tilted his body backward, shut his eyes, crossed his arms on his chest, and made believe he was about to be buried.

The sergeant, his memory refreshed, was happy to grant the visitor his wish. Opening the door, he accompanied him outside. It was the manager's impression that he could have commanded the soldiers at the rusty iron gate, even the old sergeant himself, to carry out any order he gave them if only he had been able to speak their language. At the very outset of his military career, when given his first squad command, he was aware of exerting a sober authority that raised his troops' morale. But although he was a natural leader, he also managed to convey to his superiors that there was nothing in the world he thought worth being killed for in battle. Little wonder he'd never got far in the army.

The scaly rime was gone from the coffin, and its metal surface was visible again. He touched it to see how cold it was. Not knowing at which ends the corpse's head and feet were, he positioned himself between them, reached for his phone, and scanned the sky for stars. The clouds had blurred their pinpoints. Pulling out the phone's antenna, he dialled the number of the owner from memory.

It was the middle of the night in Jerusalem. However, a man who stayed cozily at home while his personnel manager atoned for his inhumanity had to accept being wakened at odd hours.

"It's me . . ."

"Well, well! At last."

"I know this may be an intrusion, not only on your sleep,

but on your dreams. Still, I thought it best to talk to you in private, with no one else around."

"You needn't apologize, young man. At my age, sleep is a waste of time. I'm happy to hear from you at any hour."

"I didn't want that weasel of a journalist you put on my tail to overhear our conversation."

"You're right. It's best to keep your distance from him. I wouldn't spend too much time worrying about him, though. He's seeking atonement for himself. The editor promised he'll be more sympathetic this time."

"It's almost morning here, sir."

"I'm aware of the difference in time. I've been trying to follow your strange escapade on the map ... "

"I see you already know everything."

"No one knows everything. It's enough to know the main points. When I saw yesterday that you were keeping radio silence, I phoned our consul. She told me you had decided to turn your mission into an expedition."

"What was your reaction?"

"I've known of your fondness for adventure since your days as a travelling salesman, but I had no idea that your guilt towards that woman was so great."

"You're wrong, sir. It's compassion I feel, not guilt. Not just for her, but for her son. He insisted at the airport that his grandmother attend the funeral ... and since we couldn't bring her to us, I thought, as long as we're here anyway, why not give this woman what our overburdened government can't afford and bring her home to her native village at our expense? That's the proper ending for this story."

The old man sighed. "Who knows what is or isn't proper? Or whether your ending will really be the end? But what's done is done. The consul has described the fair-haired boy who put you up to it."

"He didn't put me up to anything. I felt sorry for him. He's a lonely youngster whose father treats him like a stranger. And he has the legal right to decide where his mother will be buried."

"Yes, I know all that. The consul isn't sparing of words. Or of details and commentaries. I know about your armoured vehicle, too, and about the battery you couldn't charge. Not to mention her magnificent husband whom she can't stop praising . . ."

"He's an excellent fellow."

"Well, she misses him. I believe she's jealous that he's minding you instead of her. By the way, what does she look like, this consul?"

"A giraffe."

"That's just what I thought. She talked on and on. I can't remember all she said."

"Let's stick to the point, then. We're in the middle of a long trip and can't back out. There's no way of knowing how much it will cost."

"I've already told you the expenses don't concern me."

"I am not the only one who feels guilty, sir, am I?"

"If that's how you wish to interpret my generosity, so be it. Just don't worry about money. You have unlimited credit."

"Things are very cheap here, but they still have a way of adding up."

"I'm relying on your judgment . . . on your instincts."

"Don't rely on them too much, sir. My intuition has taken to dreaming. Are you awake enough to listen to a wonderful dream I had?"

The old man seemed to shudder. "No! Your phone costs too much to dream over it. You were told to go on a short mission. If it turns out to be a longer one, that's fine with me. Just don't go off on any tangents . . ."

"We're already on one."

"How's that?"

"A minor one. To a former army base that's now a tourist site."

"What kind of base?"

"A nuclear command post from the Cold War. Our drivers heard great things about it and decided to use our rest time for an educational tour."

"You're talking to me from a nuclear command post?"

"No. We haven't visited it yet. We'll do that in the morning. I'm out in the open now, next to the coffin. It's cold, but not unbearable. I'm facing east because the dawn has planted a rosy kiss there."

"A rosy kiss?"

"Actually, the mist makes it pink."

"Watch out, young man, watch out! You're leaving me more worried than I was at the beginning of this conversation. Don't go off on any more tangents or tours at my expense. And remember, that woman won't last forever, not even in the cold."

"Don't worry. I haven't forgotten her. We have a document from the Pathology Institute that says we have lots of time."

"Listen!" The old man's apprehension was growing by the minute. "Don't rely on any documents. Trust your instincts. And remember that you're an emissary, not a general. I want you to stay in close touch with me from now on. And don't waste your battery on foolish conversations, yours or anyone else's."

6

At first he thought he had identified the exact point at which the sun would rise – a bare, snow-covered crag between two rounded hills – because the rosy glow was brightest there. Yet the loitering sun surprised him by appearing far away, from behind a distant mountain, flooding the wooded valley with a cloudy yellow light.

If the ground I'm standing on, thought the human resources manager, is one big nuclear shelter, there must be visible or concealed air vents. Looking for them, he noticed instead, beyond some distant trees, silhouettes and smoke. These belonged, he saw as he approached, to a group of vendors or gypsies setting up a market in a clearing. Was it for local inhabitants or tourists? Or might it be – but why not? – solely for him, the utter stranger, an emissary from afar who had risen early because he feared another dream?

Slowly, he made his way through the trees. Although the appearance of a mute foreigner caused the stall holders to pause in what they were doing, this did not keep him from inspecting the merchandise they had taken from their sacks and crates. The still-fresh memory of his dream of their countrywoman, whom he was returning to her native soil, was like a protective bubble around him. He strolled past heaps of potatoes, carrots, and winter squashes, red-rinded cheeses, pink, skinned suckling pigs, furry rabbits in their cages, freshly baked rye breads of different shapes and sizes, old household utensils, glasses, plates, embroidered tablecloths, linens, colourful dresses, icons, statuettes of saints. Smells of cooking enveloped him.

Only now did he notice, by signs glimpsed through their scarves and heavy coats, that most of the vendors were women. Now some smiled at him and softly called out their wares. Although he had no local currency, he was certain they would accept anything he offered.

But what should he buy? What was typical of the region? Perhaps he should wait for the consul's husband to help him tell the real from the fake. Meanwhile, he would have something to eat – something hot, even scalding, to fortify him against the death that had hovered in his dream. At the far end of the clearing, steam rose from a large pot. A woman of uncertain age, wearing a tatty fur coat, stirred the pot while singing hoarsely to herself. He couldn't be sure whether she was retarded or belonged to some exotic Arctic race. Next to her, swaddled like a gift package, a baby lay on a thick woollen blanket. What did its sweet little face, peering from beneath its bonnet, remind him of?

The emissary, lured by an excess of initiative to the ends of the earth, recalled how five days previously he had followed his secretary's baby as it scuttled down the corridor and rapped with its dummy on the old owner's door, so that he'd had to scoop it up in a quick embrace. If only he could touch the reality of the warm little body in front of him long enough to shake off his dream! Yet as no mother would lend her baby to a mute stranger, he took out a bill and pointed to the dark contents of the pot, which appeared to be some kind of stew.

The woman gave him a worried look. Muttering something, she refused to take the money. But Tartar stew was what he wanted and he laid the bill down insistently, reached for a metal mug by the pot, and handed it to her to fill. There was a warning buzz from the vendors around her – for her or for him, he couldn't tell. Since she continued to hesitate, he dipped the mug in the pot himself and slowly downed the thick liquid. Although he knew from the first sip that he was drinking an unusual brew, he went on draining it for its warmth. I needn't worry, he told himself. I ate all kinds of swill in the army and was none the worse for it.

Peasants and stall holders had surrounded him, gawking as he emptied the mug. Some were scolding the woman and trying to overturn her pot. Yet she did not seem intimidated. Brandishing an iron ladle, she kept them at bay while laughing heartily and breaking into a little song. The human resources manager, regarding her more closely, decided that she suffered from Down's syndrome.

Well, he thought, comfortingly, *even if she fed me carrion, I'll puke it up in the end. But the baby is a lost cause. I can't play with it in front of all these anxious women. It's time to move on.*

Several women followed close behind him. Although he could feel their fear on the back of his neck, he made no sense of it. Quickening his pace, he hammered on the iron gate. The soldiers recognized him and let him in, shutting the gate behind him.

He swallowed it before we understood what he wanted. There was no way to warn him because he couldn't speak our language. That's why we followed him, to tell the soldiers he had to throw up. The problem is that they don't open the gate any more unless you have a ticket. What an army! Our parents worked themselves to the bone digging a shelter for the imbeciles who ran this country, and now we have to pay to visit it!

What will happen to him now? He doesn't know what he's eaten or who made it. In the end they'll accuse us of poisoning him and shut down the market. We were too kind to that madwoman, all because of her baby. No more! You've made a mockery of us long enough, you lunatic! Say goodbye to your pot and your fire and take your baby that doesn't know its father and go sing to it by the lake. And watch out that some wolf or fox doesn't eat it by mistake.

At first he thought the stew had a fishy saltiness. Then it was a cloying sweetness. Furtively, so as not to offend the guards, he spat on a rock. His spittle, though tasting like blood, was green.

I should have swallowed it more slowly, he scolded himself. Nevertheless, he had faith in his digestive system. When all the cooks in the army had failed to poison him, how could a market vendor succeed?

The old sergeant was still at his post outside the barracks, making tea on a kerosene burner. The human resources manager, grateful for the charging of his battery, nodded hello. Although he would have liked to wash the nauseating taste from his mouth with some hot tea, he thought it best to rejoin the sleeping travellers.

Either their sleep was dreamless or their dreams were very quiet. The manager put a finger to his lips to warn the consul not to disturb them. "Everything's fine," he whispered reassuringly, though the consul did not look in need of re-assurance. Drawing a curtain on the window to keep out the morning light, he went to his corner, covered the bare feet of the boy with an unthinking movement, lay down on his mattress, bundled up in two blankets, and hoped for a dream-less sleep himself.

In fact, he had no dreams. He had only a terrible, stabbing pain, as if someone were hacking at his intestines. Three hours later he awoke, jumped to his feet, and doubled over. Fortunately – it was late and the daylight was bright – there was no one else there, because the needs of his body had overcome its inhibitions and he had fouled his pants and bedding. He was barely able to stagger to the bathroom. It was a dismal WC without a toilet seat or window, its only toilet paper strips of old newspapers, and once there he had an attack of chills. Filthy and shivering, he writhed on the cold concrete floor, not caring that the door was unlocked.

As though the woman he had fallen in love with in his dream had passed on her condition to him, he felt more dead than alive. Yet despite his agony, he could still laugh at himself. I'm obviously not a general, he thought, because even a squad leader would know enough to lock the door before deciding what to do about this mess. Still, I'm in a foreign country and will never meet anyone from it again, so what do I care? Let the journalist and the photographer see the state I'm in, too. Take a good look, you weasel. It's the Eros of your *Symposium*, a thick-skinned, unwashed *daimon* linking the human to the divine, the temporal to the eternal . . .

He didn't even try to reach the sink. It was as if getting to his feet would make him responsible for himself when all he wanted was to be a helpless baby whose mother would change his soiled clothes.

As an officer, he had seen enough cases of food poisoning in his troops to know that this one had only just begun. The blithely swallowed stew had not yet had its last word. He mustn't leave the bathroom before he was sure he could control his bodily functions. Exhausted and in shock, he stripped off his pants and underpants and lay shaking and half-naked, waiting to see what his body would do next.

A long while passed before he heard the door handle rattle. Not knowing which was worse, being found by a stranger or by someone he knew, he looked up to see, in a patch of light framed by the doorway, the Tartar boy. The light eyes beneath the pilot's cap observed him with a maturity beyond their years. Although he knew the young man had wiped all knowledge of Hebrew from his mind, he addressed him in it firmly to explain that, as bizarre as it seemed, he was looking at a case not of insanity but only of food poisoning, for which a doctor had to be summoned at once.

The boy did not, as might have been expected, run to the consul, who was enjoying a hearty breakfast in the hotel dining room. Rather, he went to get the old sergeant. A quick look at the half-naked emissary on the bathroom floor was all the sergeant needed. Leaving at once, he came back a few minutes later with three soldiers and a stretcher. They rolled the sick man onto it, where he lay like a wet, filthy rag; covered him with blankets; and carried him to a service elevator that slowly descended to the hospital deep in the ground.

The sergeant's quick response, taken without consulting his commanding officer, was not just the consequence of his natural sympathy for the emissary, whose paratrooper's boots bespoke a military past. The opportunity to perform an emergency manoeuvre in a base degraded by tourists appealed to him equally. True, the underground hospital was no longer what it had been. Less military activity meant fewer medical problems, and those who suffered from them nowadays preferred the civilian hospital in a nearby town. Why take one's chances with a questionable army medic in the bowels of the earth?

Hence, the hospital's burned-out light bulbs had not been replaced, its leaky taps continued to leak, and its central heating had been despaired of long ago. Yet its emergency lights still functioned, a legacy of the Cold War, and the sergeant was able to find his way around. Knowing that food poisoning needed no antidotes, only time to purge the system, he ordered his men to place a bed, equipped with two large chamber pots for sudden exigencies, near the toilet. Then he removed the blankets, took off the last of the emissary's clothes, and cleaned him carefully with wet washcloths. The boy, the emissary rejoiced to see, did not shrink from lending a helping hand and even wiped his feet with a cloth. What an irony, he thought. We all said he would have to bathe at our first stop, and now he's bathing me.

But what was the emissary to wear? His dirty clothes needed to be laundered and there was little point in wasting fresh ones on a man in his condition. At each new attack he jumped to his feet, determined to reach the toilet in time, only to leave telltale traces on the floor. The old sergeant, well aware of the danger, put his troops on full sanitary alert, took a torch and followed its beam to the maternity ward, and came back with some towelling nappies, faded but clean, that had been meant for Cold War infants born in a nuclear heat wave.

The mortified emissary fought with the soldiers in silence. The sergeant and his men were still swaddling him when the boy, who did not seem daunted by the sight of the struggling adult, laid a white hand on his forehead and said in Hebrew:

"No worry . . . is all nothing."

The words calmed him enough to let the soldiers finish knotting the loose ends. He even smiled back without correcting the boy's grammar.

Now that the nappy was in place, the emissary was made to drink some stale underground water to prevent dehydration. The blankets were then piled back on top of him until they formed a small mountain.

The situation was under control. The troops were dismissed and the boy was sent to inform the travellers. The sergeant appeared to regard the sick man as his personal responsibility. Drawing up a chair by the bed, he filled a humpbacked little pipe and sat awaiting the next eruption.

It was not long in coming – and it came with unanticipated ferocity. The sergeant kept calm. He changed the nappy and cleaned the patient, by now too exhausted to offer any resistance. The emissary's head weighed a ton and his eyes shut of their own accord.

It was in this position that the consul, who had interrupted his breakfast, found him. Listening in astonishment to the story of the stew, he was soon joined by the two journalists. The human resources manager lay so passively that he would not even have protested had they photographed him in his nappy for the weekly.

Yet nothing could have been further from their minds, which were elsewhere, dwelling on the immense underground shelter the travellers had just visited. Had fortifications like these, they argued between themselves, allowed the old regime to be brutal and aggressive – or had they been, on the contrary, demonstrations of weakness and fear? Room after dark room and row upon row of hospital beds lay beyond a door that the old sergeant had left open. As obsolete and rusty as the medical equipment was now, it had been sophisticated in its day, designed for every eventuality. The photographer could hardly be blamed for snapping pictures with abandon until the sergeant lunged at him, snatched the camera from his hands, removed its lens, and stuck it in his pocket.

The day passed slowly. The educational detour was taking longer than anticipated. The sick man was allowed only clear liquids. The general opinion was that anyone who had swallowed poison with such alacrity deserved to go on lying underground, wearing a nappy, flanked by two chamber pots. In any case, he wasn't alone. The old sergeant sat by him and took care of him.

8

Watched over by the sergeant, the emissary surrendered to the chills and spasms that wracked his body. *If I've actually poisoned myself out of love for a dead woman*, the feverish thought passed through his mind, *it's time to take a break and let others look after me*.

Since military permission was needed to descend to the underground hospital, a schedule of shifts was set up. Satisfied that the nappies were doing their job, the sergeant let the consul relieve him and went off to rest. The human resources manager, having grown so fond of the ex-farmer that he felt like his lost cousin, gave his tiredness free rein and sank into a profound stupor intensified by the subterranean depths.

Two hours later, his innards torn by a savage new pain that sent him running in a daze to the bathroom, he noticed that the shifts had changed again. The consul was gone, his place taken by the photographer – who, sitting in the shadows by a coal brazier that had been brought to give heat, regarded the emissary's writings with disinterest. "Is there anything I can do for you?" he asked perfunctorily, after the sick man had cleaned himself, changed his own nappy, and crawled back under his blankets.

"No, thanks, I can manage. Actually, you could bring me some water. I don't want to dehydrate."

The photographer rose slowly and filled a glass with stale water. Instead of handing it to the sick man, he placed it on a table by the bed as if afraid of catching his poisoning.

"Would you mind feeling my forehead to see if I have a temperature?"

The photographer shrank back. "I wouldn't rely on me. You should ask for a thermometer."

In their day and a half of travelling together, this was the first time the two of them had been alone. The human resources manager noticed that the photographer was older than he had thought, perhaps even as old as himself.

"I'm sorry they took your lens away," he said, trying his best to break the ice. "You could have photographed me in a nappy, surrounded by chamber pots. It would have made a better cover picture than the boy."

"What makes you say that?"

"It would have shown your readers what you put me through."

"What you've been through is of no interest to our readers," the photographer declared dryly. "You'd have to croak to make the front cover."

"Well, well! I see it's no accident that you teamed up with a weasel."

"It's he who teamed up with me."

"What does the boy have that I don't? His good looks?"

"His mother. It's she who should be on the cover. We simply don't have a decent shot of her."

The human resources manager shivered under his blankets.

"I'm warning you too. Don't you dare open the coffin."

"Calm down. No one is opening anything. You shouldn't aggravate yourself when you're sick."

"I'd like to ask you something. You're a professional photographer with a practised eye ... what's so special about her face ... or for that matter, about his? Why are we attracted to them? There's something about the eyes ... an arch of some kind ... do you think it's a racial feature?"

"No, it's not that," the photographer said with confidence, as if he had already considered the matter. "It bothered me, too. That's why I kept shooting the boy until I figured it out. It's an epithelial fold in the corner of the eye. And the high cheekbones add to the illusion ... "

"Interesting," the sick man murmured. "I can see that you've thought about it."

The photographer rose to warm his hands at the brazier. "You didn't really think our readers would prefer the smell of your nappy to such a face, did you?"

The manager blushed. With a friendly smile the photographer said:

"I hope you're not offended."

"Offended? Of course not. Just pray that the sergeant gives you back your lens in time for the funeral."

"Don't worry. I have a backup camera. The main thing is for you to get better so that we can move on."

The sergeant arrived with a pitcher of tea. The shifts changed again. Now it was the turn of the elder brother, who arrived with the emissary's carry-on bag and the leather suitcase.

"You didn't have to bring them," groaned the resource manager, who was in too much pain to make himself understood. "The suitcase isn't mine anyway."

This is totally absurd, he thought. *Here I am hospitalized in an obsolete nuclear shelter, wearing nothing but a nappy, looked after by people I can't speak to, lying in light that's too dark to read by and too bright to sleep in.* He rose rebelliously, went to his bag, and took out a track suit and a sleeping pill. Donning the track suit over the nappy, he swallowed the pill. In case of another attack, the cramps, he hoped, would wake him in time. Helped by the elder brother, he detached the emergency light by his bed, added another blanket to the pile, and tried falling asleep again.

He awoke too late. Once more he was soiled and soaking wet. Not even the soldier on duty, fast asleep by the brazier, could help him. Time, which had congealed in these depths during the Cold War, turning to a grey sludge between the concrete walls, had now also ceased to flow for the sick man. Had he imagined it or had he really been given a glass of tea by the consul and promised that he would be as good as new in twenty-four hours, as happened with cows, horses, sheep, and goats? And had the weasel, coming to discuss his dissertation in the middle of the night, actually spoken of the *daimon*, whose love was more than any woman would want to endure?

Once their journey resumed, he would perhaps find out who had sat by his bed and who had been an hallucination. One way or another, when the sleeping pill wore off and he woke again, weak and drenched in sweat, the ghostly light in the windowless, timeless room heralding no known hour of the day, he knew he was over it. He was purged not only of the poisonous stew from the market but also of many older, forgotten toxins too, going back to his school years and the army.

He undid the last nappy and tossed it into the bag by his bed. Then he cleaned himself one last time and added his track suit to the bag. All out of fresh clothes, he opened a package brought by the sergeant. In it was an assortment of army trousers, shirts, and underwear, bequeathed by unknown soldiers discharged long ago. Picking items that looked his size, he slipped snugly into them. When the soldier sleeping by the bed opened his eyes, he was astonished to see the sick tourist transformed into a private in the Maintenance Corps.

The emissary, who had a normal human talent for displaying pain and misery, now deliberated how best to convey his return to health. In the end, he raised both arms high with a triumphant grin. The soldier understood at once. Since he was forbidden to free the patient without permission, however, he had to go and ask the sergeant.

Thoroughly clean and totally void, the human resources manager asked to go on a tour of the shelter before leaving it. With his satellite phone in the deep pocket of his fatigue pants he strolled through the huge rooms of the hospital. In the spectral light he saw unused blankets lying folded on virgin mattresses piled on rusting iron beds. He entered an operating theatre in which no operation had ever been performed and opened and closed drawers of medicines until, in one of them, he found an astonished little mouse staring at him.

If such a tiny creature going about its business could penetrate the hidden fastness of a nuclear shelter, he thought, could not an ethereal sound wave do the same? Taking the phone from his pocket, he decided to put it to the test.

He had no idea whether it was day or night in this place, much less in Jerusalem. Who could he call there? Certainly not the old owner. Nor the office manager. Nor his own secretary. Not even his mother, whom the story of his illness would only frighten. That left his daughter. Surely he had the right to wake her if her young voice was what the doctor ordered.

The call went through amazingly quickly. The voice at the other end was as clear beneath the ground as it would have been from a mountaintop. It was not his daughter's, however, but his ex-wife's. Wide awake and relaxed, she spoke softly. To his surprise, she did not hang up on him.

"It's me ... "

"Yes, I can hear that. What's wrong? You don't sound so well."

"I'm not." He was touched by how intimately she still knew him. "Not entirely ... "

"What's the matter?"

"I had food poisoning. But I'm better now."

"Who poisoned you?"

He laughed. "No one. I poisoned myself. I'm better."

"You always thought you had a cast-iron stomach. It's time you learned you have your limits."

"You're right. It is time."

"You're better?"

"Yes. I'm getting over it. I had a rough day. I was a wreck. But I'm better."

"It takes time. Watch what you eat. It's best just to drink. A lot."

"I'm drinking. Thank you."

"For what?"

"For worrying about me."

"I'm not worrying about you. I'm feeling sorry for you."

"That's something, too. Thank you for feeling sorry, then."

"I don't feel as sorry as all that. You don't deserve it."

"Thank you anyway. It's nice to hear you being patient. Could I ask you to do me a favour and wake our daughter? I need to hear her voice."

"You've forgotten that it's Monday. She starts school early today. She's already left."

"She has? What time is it?"

"Seven. What happened to you? I've known you to lose track of many things before, but never of time."

"You're right. The soldiers who took care of me after I collapsed took my watch and haven't returned it yet. And there's not a ray of sunlight where I am."

"Where are you?"

"Buried underground. I'm in a nuclear shelter that's also a tourist site."

"*You're* buried underground? I thought you went to bury a woman."

"Yulia Ragayev? She's still above ground. We're taking her to her mother."

"While doing some sightseeing. I thought you were in a big rush ... "

"Because of the ... corpse? We have time. There's no need

to worry. There are medical procedures nowadays. It's not what you imagine."

"I'm not worrying or imagining anything. I couldn't care less. I simply don't understand why you had to travel so far because of some dumb newspaper article. You could have buried her in Jerusalem. It's probably what she would have wanted."

"So now you know what she would have wanted. Perhaps you do care after all . . . "

"I do not! Let's drop it. I've had enough of your wisecracks. I'm sorry I ever mentioned her . . . Wake up! Who is she to me? Who are you? What do you want? Poisoned or not, go away. Do what you want. Go touring with corpses. Just leave me in peace."

9

Without waiting for their lunch, the seven travellers boarded the armoured vehicle, which coughed and shook vigorously before emitting a puff of blue exhaust and lurching from its place with a happy growl. The coffin, its ropes reinforced by a metal cable, bumped along behind it. It was the human resources manager himself who had given the order to depart. Although he'd emerged pale and weak from the depths, a long look at his folded mattress in the empty barracks room from which his two disturbing dreams had vanished – leaving him fancy-free – had convinced him to continue his mission. The consul moved the boy to the front seat, cleared a space amid the luggage for the emissary to lie in, and even coaxed him to wear his wife's red woollen cap as a head-warmer and general restorative.

Since the army base had no laundry service, the emissary had to go on wearing the second-hand army uniform in place of his own clothes. It was added to the moderate bill he received for their lodging, meals, and tour, which he augmented with a tip for all the nappies, hot tea, and sympathy. As before, the sergeant did not want to take the money. His military pride, he told the consul, would not allow it. But when his troops assailed him for his stubbornness, he flushed, gave the emissary a military salute, shut his eyes tight, and let the money be placed in his hand. The photographer, his lens restored, could not resist popping a flashbulb.

As they climbed slowly back out of the valley, now splendidly lit by a radiant noonday sky, the travellers were better able to appreciate the unique spot they had been in. Hidden in darkness on their arrival, the nuclear shelter's illusion of pastoral beauty was now visible through the vehicle's windows. The woods, the simulated quarry, the artificial lake, and the rows of red-roofed houses below them were all camouflage.

The elder brother could read the landscape as closely as a bedouin reads the desert. Once they reached the top of the mountains encircling the valley and started down the other side, towards the junction at which they had left the main road, he pointed out the stroke of luck their detour had been, despite the emissary's illness. Apart from providing them with rest and good food, it had enabled them to escape the storm that had pursued them to this very junction. Uprooted trees and fallen road signs testified to the ferocity of the assault that had blown itself out in the expanse still ahead of them.

It was this expanse, with its forests and rivers, that they now had to cross. Neither of the two brothers was familiar with it. Although they had consulted the soldiers and been given a good military map, there was no knowing if they would be able to cover ground as quickly as they had done in their journey's first stage.

Night fell. The darkness didn't matter; the real problem was the frequent crossroads, whose signs had vanished in the storm or quite simply been turned around. Still, they had no choice but to press on. Their detour had taken longer than they had planned. The old grandmother could well have returned to her village by now and heard about her daughter's death, the details of which she had a right to know as soon as possible.

As they drove farther into the night, they were surprised to discover that they were in a populated area. On the first leg of their journey, they had met no other traffic. Now, however, they occasionally passed a slow-moving truck or had to pull onto a shoulder to let a speeding car flash drunkenly by. Once, they stopped for two horses whose harness had become entangled in a wagon shaft. Another time, a large cow blocked the road. To their astonishment they even encountered another vehicle exactly like their own. It might have come from the same assembly line or even the same armoured brigade, the only difference being that this one had been turned into a mobile home and its trailer into a kitchen.

From time to time they drove through a town or village. Despite the late hour, the inhabitants were awake and friendly and ready to give and even draw directions. The news that the coffin had come from Jerusalem and was now on its way to the birthplace of a woman killed in someone else's war caused a stir. More than one local resident doffed his cap and crossed himself as if in the presence of a sacred relic. Their warm reception encouraged the elder brother to listen to the advice of a gas station attendant to take a shortcut through a forest. By following it, he was told, they would reach the river crossing early in the morning in time to make the first ferry, an icebreaker that did not run at night.

It was nearly dawn when the driver, with the help of the attendant's drawing, found the beginning of the shortcut. As exhausted as they were, they decided after a brief debate to set out on it. It was a dirt road strewn with twigs and branches, over which the vehicle crunched pleasantly.

It was still crunching when the sleeping travellers awoke to find themselves in milky daylight, in a forest whose branches were matted with a parasitical growth that hung in long, dull beards; snarled and tangled, these sickly curtains made it hard to see what lay ahead. The drivers were in constant danger of getting lost. Far from a shortcut, the forest now seemed like a huge creature that threatened to strangle them. The road, clearly marked at the outset, forked every several hundred metres, forcing them to choose.

The younger brother drove. The elder brother sat beside him. The travellers had never seen him so pale and tense. He held the map in one hand and a compass in the other, and both hands shook each time he said "left" or "right". The route indicated by the compass did not always look correct; often it was the narrower or more rutted of the choices and caused the coffin to jounce wildly. Although the vehicle performed well, its big chassis, springs, and powerful engine a tribute to the engineer who designed it, their navigator's growing anxiety that they might be on a wrong course, a course that would leave them stranded among the trees like another parasite, infected them all.

Each retreated into his own heavy silence: that of the consul, who until now had never lacked words and had served as a bridge between the locals and the foreigners, was the hardest to cope with. Yet the emissary was determined to respect it. Feeling hunger for the first time since his poisoning, he rose from his litter, found a baked potato, and gnawed at it with a steady appetite. He was facing backwards, looking out at the profuse matted clusters that brushed the woman's coffin. How had he ever been foolish enough to agree to make her his business?

Several nerve-racking hours went by. At last, the lacka-daisical sun, after blinking on and off through the trees, shone for an instant on a broad band of clear horizon. At once they set the vehicle on a course for it.

The attendant's advice had been correct after all. The shortcut not only existed but had brought them to their destination – not a moment too soon, since the frozen river's banks, between which the ferry plied a channel, were already crowded with people. Men, animals, cars, and wagons were waiting to cross to the opposite side, on which another multi-tude was waiting to cross back.

This was the river that had been mentioned to him by the consul – whether as a challenge, an obstacle, or a memorable experience – on his first day in the provincial capital. Frozen into a white glaze, it was solid enough to walk or play on. The elder brother, after parking their vehicle in line, was overcome with relief at being rescued from circling endlessly in the forest. A shy man unaccustomed to displaying emotion, he left the group and strode out onto the ice. By the time he reached the middle of it, he was no more than a dot on the white surface. There, as if suddenly hit by lightning, he fell to his knees and struck his head on the ice in thankful exaltation.

Once more a market had sprung up, a small one in the middle of all the people, vehicles, wagons, horses, cows, and pigs. If nothing else, it helped everyone to bargain away the time while waiting for the ferry. The consul, however, his red cap back on his head, feared a repeat of the emissary's illness. Nothing that he did not personally authorize, he told the travellers, was to be eaten by them.

The daylight was fading. The coffin, it seemed, would not cross before morning; they would be marooned by the river for the night. The consul decided to throw himself on the mercy of the crowd. Taking the young boy with him, he circulated through it, stopping repeatedly to tell the tragic story of the dead woman going home to her old mother. The simple narrative had its effect, as did the boy's handsome looks. The unyielding line relented and gave way, letting the coffin and its armoured escort proceed.

They boarded the ferry at dusk, on its last crossing of the day. A glorious sunset lit their way. Over the objections of the consul, who had lost his easygoing attitude since the poisoning, the human resources manager decided to cross the ice on foot and asked the photographer to record the event for his daughter. The journalist, unwilling to be bested, decided to join him. They walked cautiously, doing their best to keep their footing, while the photographer climbed on the coffin to get a better shot.

"If the ice breaks now," grinned the pudgy journalist as they heard a suspicious crack beneath them, "our story will lose its hero and its author in one fell swoop. Nothing will be left but a back-page item about two adventurers who looked for trouble and found it."

"That might be just as well." The emissary's deep sorrow surprised him. "With a reputation for devotion to corpses, no living woman will want to touch me."

"I'm not so sure," the weasel said with a smile, laying a consoling hand on the shoulder he had promised to steer clear of. "You'll see that your devotion will win you many admirers. You won't have to look for them in out-of-the-way bars any more. They'll come looking for you ... and who knows, perhaps for me too ... "

10

Since hearing the bitter news from Jerusalem, which we had imagined existed only in the Bible, we couldn't stop tormenting ourselves. Holy Mother, give us the heartfelt wisdom not to err!

At once we sent a messenger to tell the old woman to come home from the monastery. We made her promise to say nothing about the tragedy. Four nights and five days went by without a word from her. Although the storm had washed away roads and knocked down bridges, we lit a bonfire every night to make sure she could find her way back.

Ah, what would we do if the dead daughter arrived before the mother was here to mourn for her? Should we bury her or wait? And if we waited, where was the most dignified place to keep her? Should we break into the old woman's cottage and put her daughter in the bed she was born in? Or should we place the coffin, as we always do for funerals, by the altar in the church? But dear Jesus, how long could we pray with a corpse lying beside the holy icons? And how could we, who are used to the dead faces of aged peasants, look into a coffin with a mangled body from Jerusalem?

And who would speak at the funeral? We hadn't seen her for years and knew nothing about her. All we had were distant memories of a quiet, delicate child who went everywhere with her mother – to the fields, to the market, to the church – until some man fell in love with her and carried her off to the big city. At first her mother used to travel all the way there to see her. She said her daughter was an engineer and had a beautiful baby. But once we were connected to the telephone

*lines, she stopped going. Could the poor woman have been in touch
with her daughter in Jerusalem without telling us?*

*For five nights we knew no peace. And then came the news that the
coffin had crossed the river on the ferry, with an armoured vehicle and
a big escort — and still no sign of the mother. What were we to do?
What were we to tell the delegation that was bringing us an engineer
who had died as a cleaning woman in someone else's war?*

Holy Mother, we asked and asked and got no answers.

*And so, when the big wheels came to a halt by our fire, we didn't
know what to believe. We even hoped that the coffin might be empty
and that your silence had foretold a miraculous resurrection. For a
second, but no more, we actually thought that was her climbing down
from the vehicle, as young and beautiful as ever. But as we approached
in joy and trembling, we saw that it was only her son, a tall boy who
had brought his mother home to his grandmother for her to turn
despair and anger into sorrow and pity.*

*It was a distinguished delegation. Its armoured vehicle was so big
and old that it needed two drivers, and its story was so long that it
needed two journalists, and even its leader needed someone to interpret
what he said.*

*At first we didn't know that the white-faced man in the old army
uniform was the leader. But he was a man without guile and we
understood as soon as he spoke, Holy Mother, that he was the answer
to all our questions.*

This is what he said:

*Villagers do not fear the passing of time. The body of your fellow
villager has returned to you embalmed like an Egyptian princess.
Therefore, be in no hurry to bury her. Time will stop and wait
patiently for her mother to return and bid her farewell. If you are
afraid to lay her in her childhood bed, or in the church, and to pray
next to a corpse which is neither a statue nor an icon, put her in the
school in which she studied as a young girl, because that is where we
all waited for our own mothers. And when it is time for her funeral,
know that she has been brought back to you as whole and unblemished
as a sleeping angel and do not fear to lift the lid of her coffin.*

*As for me, I am not a messenger who comes and goes. I am a
human resources manager whose duty it is to remain with you until*

the last clod of earth has fallen on my employee's grave, before returning to the city which is for me only a bitter reality.

II

The peasants, though reluctant at first to put a coffin in a schoolhouse, quickly came to the conclusion that it was the most logical and reasonable place. One way or another, the delegation needed a place to sleep, and so the villagers decided to give the children a few days off school. Anything to avoid leaving an untended coffin in their midst.

The ropes were untied and the coffin was moved from the trailer to the teachers' room, the door of which was firmly locked. The tables and chairs were pushed together in the classrooms, the floors were covered with fresh straw, from the houses came mattresses, blankets, and pillows, and the delegation was soon ensconced in the little schoolhouse. Calm returned to the village. A few peasants remained by the bonfire, so they could greet the returning pilgrim, who they feared might by now have an inkling of what awaited her.

Yet the messenger managed to bring the old woman back without arousing her suspicion. In fact, so uplifted was she by her visit to the monastery, with all its prayers and masses for the New Year, that she returned wearing clerical robes and a monk's hood. When the human resources manager, the consul, and her grandson were hurriedly brought to her late at night, they were startled to be confronted by a round little monk with kind eyes and a gentle voice.

The villagers, it seemed, had lacked the fortitude to inform her of her daughter's cruel death and had left it to the emissary to break the news, with the full authority of the company – indeed, of the entire city of Jerusalem – behind him. First, though, they had tactfully presented the old woman with her grandson. Although she had not seen him for years, she recognized him at once and understood that something grave must have happened to have brought him from afar. At once she tore off her hood, revealing in full the original face from which such a captivating pair of copies had been made.

The frightened boy was already regretting the journey he had insisted on. Pointing to the schoolhouse in which his mother lay, in a stammering voice he told his grandmother of the Jerusalem bombing. The shocked old woman grasped it all immediately. Yet it was not just the grandson's story that shocked her. She was also aghast at the idea that the body of her daughter had been transported all this way for no good reason. Why, she asked angrily, had the dead woman not been given a funeral in the city she had chosen to live in, in Jerusalem? It was her city. It was everyone's.

"Everyone's?" The emissary whispered the word wonderingly to the consul. "In what way?"

"In no way," the consul snapped, baring a temper he had kept concealed until now. Without asking for the opinion of the human resources manager, he sternly explained that Jerusalem was out of the question.

The old woman reacted like a wounded animal. Sensing that the delegation's true captain was not the elderly man with the silver curls but the younger one in the uniform with the pallid face and weary eyes, she threw herself heartrendingly at his feet, pleading that her daughter be returned to the city that had taken her life. That way, she, too, the victim's mother, would have a right to it.

The grandson was bewildered by this unexpected appeal. He bent to pull the old woman to her feet, only to be pushed angrily away. Sprawling in bitter grief in the dirt by the campfire, she all but rolled on its coals. Several villagers had to seize her and bring her back to her cottage. Her feet barely touched the ground as they carried her; she seemed to skim through the air.

The human resources manager felt devastated at having been the bearer of doubly disappointing tidings. All his good intentions – all his daring generosity – had led to a completely unintended result. Perhaps, he suggested, the consul might come with him to the cottage to help explain that he wasn't to blame.

For the first time since he had made his acquaintance, however, the manager could feel that the ex-farmer was hostile. Adamantly, almost insultingly, the consul rejected the request.

"That will do! We've had enough of your guilt. You've gone much too far with it. You can't involve the whole world in your obsession with a dead cleaning woman."

Coming from someone so friendly and considerate until now, this rebuke left the emissary too stunned to speak. Deeply hurt, he turned and retraced his steps towards the sleeping travellers in the schoolroom.

Near a pile of chairs and tables, not far from the blackboard, the journalist and the photographer lay wrapped in their blankets. As usual, the human resources manager thought, they've missed the critical, excruciatingly human moment. When they wake, they'll make up for it by staging some tear-jerking scene.

He looked balefully at the consul, who was spreading a blanket before crawling under it. You've forgotten that I hired you, he wanted to say. You're under contract. But thinking better of it, he took the leather suitcase and left the schoolroom.

The long northern winter night showed no sign of ending. The death having been announced and all unanswered questions answered, the peasants had dowsed the fire and gone to bed. In the morning they would prepare the church for the funeral service.

He walked along snow-covered paths, among darkened cottages. For the first time since setting out from Jerusalem, he felt the weight of his own solitude. Yet he was sure that he could find the old woman's cottage and let her know that he alone found nothing strange in her request.

A light shone in a window. That's hers, he guessed, re-minded of Yulia Ragayev's little shack in Jerusalem. Coming closer, he could see through the fogged window that the old woman was not by herself. Her grandson was at her side, and she was surrounded by friends. Although he had no way of making himself understood, he could no longer depend on the consul. He entered the cottage silently and handed the old woman the suitcase as if he and she were family and no words were necessary between them.

12

At noon he joined the consul and the two drivers in the line of villagers waiting to pass before the coffin. Something in him, however, balked. I have seen her, he thought, in my dreams – in torment, faint from weariness, but alive. I have even been tempted to love her. What need have I to see her corpse?

He silently signalled the consul and the drivers to step ahead of him. The journalist and the photographer were already inside the church and had seized the best vantage points. Although he had forbidden him to take pictures, the human resources manager was sure that the photographer would strike silently, without his flashbulb, to fill the pages between the rentals and the used-car ads. The weasel and the rattle-snake hadn't made this journey together in order to miss their true subject: the alluring face of Death.

The last villagers disappeared through the large wooden door of the church. The human resources manager did not follow them. He turned and walked down a narrow path to the little village graveyard. At its end was an ice-covered wall that seemed to mark the limits of the universe.

There wasn't a sound. He wandered past new and old tombstones, looking for a fresh grave. None was visible. The old woman must be insisting on the coffin's return to Jerusalem. Perhaps the villagers, afraid of her wrath, were planning to bury it secretly, at night.

A sound of voices reached him from the church, along with a thin, stifled wail. Then came the deep baritone of the village priest. It began with words and changed to music, to a slow, ancient, ecstatically chanted dirge. The villagers joined in, piercing the emissary to the quick. Although he knew a place of honour had been prepared for him and he would have liked to express his condolences, he was determined to remain outside. He did not want to see her, not even from a distance.

It's time to say goodbye, the human resources manager whispered, wiping away a cold, unexpected tear. He paced back and forth by the icy wall, touching it warily, while the old woman's complaint went on pursuing him. Did we make a mistake? Were we too hasty? An engineer like that doesn't come to Jerusalem just for work. She comes because she feels that the shabby city is hers too. Her Jewish lover gave up and left, and she stuck it out. If the night shift supervisor hadn't fired her out of love, she would still be working in our bakery.

He was too distraught to tell whether he was trembling from cold or excitement. If it was noon in this place, it was 10 a.m. in Jerusalem. He took out his satellite phone and dialled the company owner.

The office manager was delighted to hear the human resources manager's voice. She had been thinking of him, she said. Had he reached his destination? Was he already on his way back? Everybody was asking when he would return.

"Soon," he said softly, astonished once again by how close the phone made her sound. Right now, he needed to talk to the old man.

"Have you forgotten that it's Wednesday?" She was surprised that he hadn't remembered. "He's on his weekly tour of the bakery."

"In that case," the manager said, "put me through to him there."

"Wouldn't you rather wait until he returns to his office?"

"There's no time," he said firmly. "We have to make some decisions."

She transferred the call to the bakery. Above the old man's gnarled voice, he could hear the purring of ovens and the rattle of production lines.

"I have something urgent to discuss with you."

"Ah, my dear fellow! I've been looking forward to this

conversation. But I'm in the middle of making the rounds with the shift supervisors. Can't it wait?"

"No, sir."

"It's hard to concentrate with all this noise."

"Yes, sir, I can hear it. It doesn't bother me, because there's not a sound where I am. I'm standing by an icy wall with nothing beyond it. It feels like the end of the world. It's comforting to know that the bakery is still running. But perhaps you can't hear me."

"Don't worry about that, young man. I'm used to the sounds of the bakery. I've been hearing them since I was an infant at my parents' knees. It's like the sound of waves to a fisherman."

"Well, then, I'll get to the point. It's complicated. We have some decisions to make. The grandmother returned to the village this morning. Right now she's looking at the open coffin and confirming it's her daughter."

"I thought that might be necessary. I should have warned you that you might have to look, too."

"I didn't look at anything, sir. Nor do I intend to. There's no need. That woman is inside me by now. I even dream about her."

"As you wish, my friend. You know that I trust your intuition. When will the funeral take place?"

"That's just it. We've got to the painful part, but not to the end. You were right to worry about that. It turns out that the end hasn't ended. The old woman doesn't want to bury her daughter in the village. She's upset that we didn't bury her in Jerusalem. She says it's her city, too."

"Hers? How?"

"That's a good question. We'll have to think about it."

"But who the devil is she, this grandmother?"

"An old woman. I'd say about your age. And she's strong and stubborn like you. This morning she came back from a pilgrimage dressed as a monk. It was a sight for sore eyes."

"But what is it you want from me now?"

"I want your agreement to our bringing the cleaning

woman back to Jerusalem."

"Back to Jerusalem! How can we?"

"We can and we will. There's no choice."

"Excuse me. We have no jurisdiction. It's up to the government and National Insurance."

"The government has washed its hands of the matter. Even if we could pressure it, there is no way they can now make arrangements for the return of a dead temporary resident who believed in Jerusalem more than Jerusalem believes in itself. The two of us – you, the owner of a large company, and I, your loyal employee – may be private individuals, but with our vision and initiative . . . "

"Are you out of your mind?"

"No, sir. Not at all. It takes more than that to drive an old hand like me out of his mind. My mind couldn't be clearer. It's as clear as blue skies and a wall of ice."

"I don't understand a word you're saying. Maybe this noise is affecting my hearing after all. Please stick to the point. Are you proposing to return to Jerusalem with the coffin? How can you?"

"Why not? We have to bring the car and trailer back anyway. The aeroplane that flew us here also flies the other way. And if you're concerned about time running out – for the woman, that is – you needn't be. Time isn't running in the coffin at all. We've been assured it's been brought to a stop."

"But suppose I say no. What will you do then?"

"I'll bring her back at my own expense. I'm not a wealthy man, but I'll manage. As your human resources manager, I'm authorized to grant myself a small company loan. The question, sir, is rather: what will happen to your precious humanity? Who will restore it? Do you want the weasel to write that you backed out at the last minute?"

"Now you're threatening me."

"Threatening? Oh, no, sir. I'm your loyal employee. I'm just surprised that a man of your wisdom and experience didn't realize that a journey like this could benefit a city we've despaired of."

"Benefit how, you absurd man? With another grave?"

"Another grave and two new residents, an old woman and a handsome young man."

"You're proposing to bring them too?"

"Why not? Isn't it their right?"

"Right? Right?" The old owner's shouts drowned out the sound of the ovens. "What right are you talking about?"

"That, sir, is something we'll figure out. As always, I am at your service."

Haifa, 2002–3